The Steal
An Adventure in Montreux

Kunal Mohanlal

Kunal Mohanlal
2015

First Printing: 2015

ISBN-13: 978-0692591826 (Custom)
ISBN-10: 0692591826
BISAC: Fiction / Mystery & Detective / International Mystery & Crime

Kunal Mohanlal
2 Skytop Road
Edison, NJ 08820

Ordering Information:

Special discounts are available on quantity purchases by corporations, associations, educators, and others. For details, contact the publisher at the above listed address.

U.S. trade bookstores and wholesalers: Please contact Kunal Mohanlal
Tel: (732) 310-4080; or email kunal.mohanlal@gmail.com

Dedication

Dedicated to my charming wife Geeta and my wonderful sister Benu for their enthusiastic support on this book and other things in life! To my awesome sons Mihir and Madhav for indulging me and my ideas. A big thanks is also due to them for silently suffering the editorial burden they bore.

It was 8 am on Saturday when Jai Singh woke up to a bright, sunny June morning in Montreux, Switzerland. He was a tall, handsome and wiry man with a distinct sharp nose. He was often mistaken for an athlete as he had the ease of an outdoorsman. There was nothing flamboyant about him, but to the discerning, his elegance, gracious nature and gallantry hinted of some royal heritage.

Jai loved the town which had been his home for many years. Henri, his valet had just served coffee and from the chalet window Jai could see the small boats bobbing up and down on Lake Geneva and the large ones starting to do their rounds.

Based at the foot of the Alps, Montreux combined the lazy charm of an idyllic village with just the right buzz of social and commercial enterprise. During the day, the town bustled with tourists and in the evenings there were many social hotspots for the young or young at heart. Montreux had also distinguished itself with music lovers by hosting many events through the year.

Jai was a renowned physicist with the École Polytechnique Fédérale de Lausanne (EPFL). He did his graduate studies at EPFL and later joined the nuclear fusion research team there. On any workday his ride to Lausanne and back was normally under an hour through beautiful countryside. On the way back he sometimes stopped at the Vineyard Terraces at Lavaux to sip a glass of wine. On occasion, he carried back a bottle of Chasselas or Pinot Noir.

Jai was excited as he had to go to Geneva to pick up his step brother, Dev Singh, who was arriving from India. Dev was 27 and two years younger than him. They had much catching up to do. Even though they talked frequently on phone, Jai had not met Dev for a number of years. In fact, on Jai's last visit to India in 2014, they had missed each other as Dev was travelling to New York.

Dev had been operating a carpets business with manufacturing facilities in India. He sold the carpets locally and also to international clientele. After staying with Jai a few days, Dev would proceed to Zurich and London to attend some client meetings.

Louise, Henri's wife, was in the kitchen preparing for the day. She was plump and bubbly with twinkling eyes. She managed the cooking

3

and other household chores. Jai had already informed her that Dev would be coming in later in the day.

Louise knew that Dev especially enjoyed her preparation of Geschnetzeltes, Rösti, salat and chocolate soufflé. Jai walked over to where the dishes were cooking as the aroma was divine. Taking a few deep breaths, he said, "Mmmm this smells fantastic!" Louise beamed with pride.

Outside, the pool looked especially inviting. Jai walked across for a quick dip before breakfast. The water felt warm and welcoming and he did a few laps to build up an appetite. He knew that Louise would lay it on thick being a Saturday morning.

Henri was pottering about in the chalet gardens where the laurels, magnolias and cypress were looking lush. He had planted some rhododendrons a few days back and was checking to see how well they were holding up in the summer. He thought the plants were drooping just a little, so he sprinkled some plant food and ensured an extra round of watering around them.

The chalet, built in 1700s was set on a 5 acre property at the edge of Lake Geneva. Several additions and changes had taken place over the years. The house was like a white pearl set in verdant greens next to the deep blue lake. The garden sloped down to the water where the chalet had its own private dock and boathouse. The property offered magnificent views of the Alps to the west and south across the waters.

After his swim and change, Jai went over to the dining room. He was not surprised that Louise has prepared a large breakfast of eggs, bacon, hot freshly baked croissants and coffee. Sometimes, he thought, she pampered him even more than his mother did!

After breakfast, Jai flipped through "*24 heures*" and "Tribune de Genève" to check the headlines. There was nothing eye catching. Both papers seemed to be tracking the happenings leading up to the Montreux Jazz Festival in early July. Jai always looked forward to the event having attended almost all the festivals in the last eleven years that he had been resident in Montreux.

It was time to head to the airport. Jai's bright yellow Maserati Gran Turismo growled as he swung out of the garage – he would take Autoroute A9 and then A1 from Lausanne on his way to Geneva. The traffic on the highway was light at first but became denser after crossing Lausanne. It took him just over an hour to reach the airport. Jai parked his car and waited for Dev in the arrivals lobby, full of anticipation.

After a wait of 15 minutes or so, Jai saw his good looking brother of medium height walking out with a suitcase and a handbag. Dev always kept long flowing hair that danced around in tune with his springy gait.

The brothers were most happy to see each other and Dev gave Jai his customary bear hug. "Jai, you look 3 inches shorter – you certainly have been slogging your backside I can see," joked Dev.

"And as always you have been piling into biryani – all the extra pounds are showing," countered Jai.

"Get off, I jog 5 kilometers almost every day and have started doing yoga. Gone are the days you can outdo me on the track!" retorted Dev. Both laughed as they settled into their usual spirit of banter and camaraderie.

"Ok, tell me how is Veer doing? Lalita and the kids?" Jai asked, referring to his elder brother Veer Singh and his sister in law Lalita.

"They are well and send their love and affection," replied Dev, "Veer is expanding the hotel business and is planning to buy properties in the Far East, China and Japan. He is travelling quite a bit. He gave me a bottle of Suntory whiskey for you."

"Ok good – this way we know what we are drinking tonight," responded Jai, "unless you want to step out in the evening."

The drive back took a bit longer, but since they had so much to talk about, it did not feel like a long ride. Dev told Jai about how things were in Dhawalpur, where both had grown up. The family farming business had suffered a setback because of drought conditions but the other businesses were performing fine. His own plans to grow the carpets business in Europe was shaping up quite well.

"Veer has also renovated the Lake Palace property and has converted it into a hotel. It has come out very nicely. It's a pity that with the drought, the lake itself has shrunk to half its size," said Dev.

Jai told Dev about their sister Gauri's visit to Montreux a week ago. She and her husband Pranav had come down from Antwerp over the weekend. Pranav had been keen to showcase the *Soomjam* jewel to some friends in Geneva. The showing itself had taken place at Jai's chalet in Montreux on June 7th. *Soomjam* was a brooch, owned by Jai, with rich and notable history and had been in the Singh family for 150 years. It was gifted to him by his father on his 18th birthday shortly before he moved to Switzerland from India.

"I knew of their visit and wanted to come last week itself, but my client meetings in Zurich and London could not get coordinated," said Dev, "I will try and see if I can fly via Antwerp on my way back to India."

"Gauri will love it, if you can manage to meet her," responded Jai.

"Who attended the showing?" asked Dev, "anyone I know?"

"There were about fifteen people at the gathering. You know a few, Lady Tara Cuthbert has been to Dhawalpur, Jürgen Merz and Claude Fillon are the bankers whom you have met in Geneva last time you were in Switzerland, and Nicole Binoche from my office. Not sure if you know any of the others."

They had a late lunch and the Geschnetzeltes and soufflé were a big hit. Dev complimented Louise on the delightful food. The sincerity of his tone pleased her always. She looked forward to visits from Jai's family members. Her cottage was brimming with gifts and knick-knacks from India. This time Dev presented her with an embroidered woolen shawl from Kashmir. Louise was thrilled with the gift.

In the evening, the brothers headed to town for drinks and dinner. Since Dev was feeling somewhat jet lagged, they decided to return early after a few beers and a quick bite to eat.

Jai reclined the plush business class seat and stretched his feet forward as the jet reached cruising altitude. He had had a busy day at work but thankfully the Swiss Air flight from Geneva to Moscow took off on time. Earlier there was some concern that heavy rain and winds may delay the take off. Jai liked to watch Lake Geneva glimmer and recede into the background, but as the skies were overcast, there was not much of a view that day.

Jai pulled out his tablet and finished up some work that he was carrying with him. He was also thinking about his lecture the next day at the Russian Academy of Sciences. His research in nuclear fusion at EPFL had caught attention of the fusion community across the globe. He was considered an authority on the subject and his papers had been widely published in prominent International Atomic Energy Agency (IAEA) journals.

The promise of nuclear fusion was that given the right conditions, it had the potential to generate copious quantities of energy and hence the possibility of solving the planet's energy needs. Even though nuclear fusion research had been conducted for over fifty years, it had not yet led to self-sustaining controlled fusion reactions. One of the key constraints had been confinement of the hot plasma for which a device known as the Tokamak was used.

Jai and his team had been working on Tokamak configuration to analyze and manage turbulent structures in fusion plasmas. Recently he had made a breakthrough that would allow sustainable fusion in a commercially viable manner. The project called *Solara* was highly classified; it had participation of four countries – Switzerland, UK, France and Germany.

Jai knew that his work was being closely followed by the Russian scientific community and his lecture would provide the Russians with an overview of the outcomes being observed in *Solara*. As was customary in commercial oriented research he would not be divulging any details.

Jai was excited about his latest research and continued to mull over the findings. Other than slight choppiness, the flight had been smooth. The pilot announced that the plane was about to land at Domodedovo

International Airport in 20 minutes. Jai decided to take a taxi to the Hotel President on Bolshaya Yakimanka Street where he was planning to stay.

The main restaurant in Hotel President offered excellent cuisine to suit most palates. Jai was ravenous and ordered roast duck in spicy mango salsa. The waiter was knowledgeable about which wine to pair with the food and suggested a Viognier. After dinner, Jai decided to hit the bed as he had an early start the next day.

Jai's lecture at the Russian Academy of Sciences was very well attended as there was much interest in his research. He was quite aware that the Tokamaks were first invented by Russian scientists - another reason the attendees would be keen to learn about *Solara*. There was representation from Moscow as well as St. Petersburg, owing to the significant research ongoing in both places.

The Moscow team in the audience had been engaged in research that was quite akin to the *Solara* project but their results had not been very promising. Their leader was Leonid Batcheff and he asked Jai probing questions, but Jai's responses skirted around the specifics.

Watching the proceedings remotely via video link was Sergei Zhuk, an officer with the Scientific and Technical Service division of FSB responsible for monitoring key global developments in scientific areas including fusion research. Sergei was a seasoned veteran at FSB. He was a pale thin man with a forever angry demeanor. He had an aggressive style that he used effectively to intimidate others.

After the lecture was over, Sergei huddled with Leonid in a small chamber on the second floor of the Academy. Leonid was very keen to obtain more specifics of the work that Jai and his team were doing and was frustrated that past attempts had failed. Sergei promised that he would think of a way to get him details on the *Solara* project.

Back in his office, Sergei called Igor Primakov his contact in Geneva who had done jobs for him in the past. Since Igor was not FSB, it would help maintain anonymity about FSB's involvement and keep an arm's length in case things turned sour.

Sergei wanted Igor to use his network in Switzerland to find out more about where and how project *Solara* information was being stored.

Veer Singh was the titular Maharaja of Dhawalpur even though there was no such official title. He resided in the elegant Rangmahal palace from where his ancestors had ruled the state prior to Indian independence in 1947.

The palace was built around 1760 and was laid over 1000 acres of rolling gardens, lakes, pools and fountains. The façade was red sandstone and colored glass, while the rooms were tiled with the finest quality marble. The royal family crest comprising a tiger, horse and crossed spears was emblazoned above the palace doorway.

While the Maharajas were a thing of the past, Veer Singh still commanded respect and had an air of aristocracy about him. He was charismatic, colorful and walked with an air of authority. He did not have the royal clout of his forefathers, but thanks to his business acumen and sharp investment skills, the family wealth had grown. His business interests included properties, hotels, resorts and farming.

Jai called Veer's mobile as he was strolling in the Rangmahal palace gardens with Shera, his favorite Alsatian, and the perpetual pipe clenched between his teeth.

"Yes Jai, how are things in Montreux?" he asked.

"Veer, I am doing fine, hope Lalita, the kids and you are keeping well. You know, that we are planning a showing for *Soomjam* on June 7th when Gauri and Pranav will be here."

"Yes indeed, Gauri mentioned to me in our last conversation. Do you think a private showing at the chalet is a good idea?" asked a concerned Veer.

"This is such a safe place, I don't anticipate any trouble," replied Jai.

"Ok, at least send me a list of all those you have invited," requested Veer.

When they were done talking, Veer called a number in the UK.

Igor Primakov was a hulk of a man, with short cropped hair and huge hands that could be put to deadly effect when the need arose. He ran his set-up from Geneva under the guise of a trucking and logistics operation.

Through his inquiries, Igor learnt that the *Solara* data was stored on EFPL servers which would be difficult to hack into. But Jai was the project leader and his laptop also had a copy of the same information. Sergei instructed Igor to replicate the data on Jai's laptop.

"Sergei, why don't we just pinch his laptop?" asked Igor.

"This job needs to be done very discreetly, we do not want to expose ourselves to any diplomatic concerns," responded Sergei keeping his irritation in check. "Naturally we need to make sure that neither Jai nor anyone else should become aware that the data has been copied."

He asked Igor if there was anyone in Montreux who could do the job, someone who knew the area well.

Igor told Sergei that he had the right man in mind. Piotr Babicz had been active in the Lausanne area for a number of years. His specialty was cyber theft, stealing documents, laptops and media. He seemed to be the perfect match for this job.

Piotr Babicz was a sinewy and muscular man with street smart ways. He was in his early thirties with a furry brow and receding hairline. He was clever thief but being a tactical person he rushed into situations and did his thinking after the act. He combined traditional burglary with new techniques such as online identity theft and selling stolen personal and corporate data on the web.

Piotr was earlier based in Marseille where he and his brother Radoslaw were members of a Polish mafia called the "South Side Gang". They were responsible for smuggling cars and electronic goods to Poland. After a persistent police crackdown both had to flee Marseille. Piotr moved to Switzerland and Radoslaw went back to Poland. When things became quieter Radoslaw returned to Marseille and formed a smaller gang dealing in contraband. Piotr continued to stay in Switzerland on the outskirts of Lausanne.

Piotr's home in Aclens was 20 minutes from Lausanne, less than an hour from Geneva to the south west and Montreux to the south east. The neighborhood was quite sparsely populated providing him enough privacy to maintain unusual hours and to come and go without being noticed.

In the last several years, there had been a steady rise in corporations spying on each other. This had led to increased laptop and media theft resulting in improved business for Piotr. Depending on the situation, he could get up to twenty five thousand dollars for each job. A few weeks ago when Igor contacted him, Piotr had just concluded a laptop burglary in Thoiry, France; just across the border from Geneva. He had made twenty thousand dollars on that deal.

Igor's job had an additional complication. Piotr could not just steal the laptop from Jai Singh, he had to copy the data without leaving behind any trace. Piotr expected Igor to offer around fifty thousand dollars. He was pleasantly surprised when Igor offered him a cool hundred thousand.

In the last few weeks, Piotr had been following Jai's movements between office and home. His office at EPFL had high security so Piotr decided to carry out the data theft at the chalet. He took a few photographs of the area to plan his moves.

He was certainly tempted with other ideas seeing an expensive chalet in an affluent area of Montreux. But Igor had made it very clear that the theft had to be clean and unnoticed. Piotr was aware of Igor's reputation and ruthlessness and decided it was best to follow directions as laid out.

Based on his observations, Piotr knew that on Sunday afternoons Jai was at the club for a few hours. He had also observed that once Jai left for the club, the groundskeeper and his wife locked the chalet front door and retired to their cottage for the afternoon. He would pick either June 7th or 14th as his target date to carry out his plan.

On June 7th, Piotr noticed certain guests at the chalet and decided to execute his plan the following Sunday.

Sunday morning was going to be a lazy one. Jai and Dev enjoyed a hearty breakfast, and Louise made sure that the menu was traditional Swiss fare with gipfeli, Appenzeller cheeses, some cold cuts and soft boiled eggs. They enjoyed coffee on the terrace and watched the sun glimmer on the gentle blue waters lapping the shore.

Dev enquired, "What about your ski trip? Were you not planning for Zermatt in the next week or two?" He knew that Jai was a ski fanatic and took off for Zermatt few times every year to be on the slopes. He always drove over and it took him about 2 hours from Montreux.

"Yes, I had something planned for June 27th, let's see how it works out," responded Jai.

"And how is Sophie doing?" asked Dev.

Jai and Sophie Laffin had been together for two years but had gradually drifted apart in the past year. Jai told him that she was well, but they did not see much of each other except for a hello on the phone once in a while.

"I like her a lot you know," said Dev, "you guys should get back again."

"I know, but I think the pressure of work gets to both of us and things just don't seem to be working out," said Jai. Then changing the subject, "Do you want to come along to the club this afternoon?" he asked.

"I'll pass and catch up on my sleep so we can do something this evening," responded Dev.

At around 2 pm, Jai said goodbye to Dev and drove off for his game of tennis.

Piotr drove a nondescript dark blue Ibiza that he parked down the lane from Jai's chalet at about 1.45 pm. He took out his binoculars and a black bag containing his other equipment and moved to a vantage point where shrubs and trees provided him with good cover. A few minutes later he saw Jai drive off. Soon thereafter the groundskeeper and his wife locked the chalet front door and proceeded to their cottage.

Piotr gave it another 30 minutes just to make sure that it was safe for him to proceed. He slipped a hood over his head, and stealthily moved towards the chalet. He quickly reached the front door and took out his lock picking tools from the bag. This was a craft in which he had many years of practice. Even though the lock was of good quality, it did not offer him much resistance. He opened the door quietly, moved inside and shut it softly behind him.

He was awestruck by the rich furnishings and his eyes took in the many antiques and period furniture lying about. He had to consciously push back his desire to make away with some articles of high value.

From the lobby there was a passage leading up to the study and Piotr silently entered the room. He swiftly scanned the area and noticed Jai's office bag lying next to the study desk. He took out the laptop from Jai's bag and removed the hard disk. He attached this disk to his own laptop and copied all the contents to his own hard disk. It amazed Piotr that most people believed that their computer password provided them security against their unencrypted files being copied.

He then put Jai's hard disk back in its slot in the laptop and kept the computer away in Jai's office bag. Jai would not come to know that his data had been copied. Piotr's plan had succeeded thus far and he now needed to slip out unnoticed. He put his own laptop in his black bag and softly treaded towards the study door leading to the passage outside. As soon as he crossed the door he was shocked to see someone coming towards him.

Dev had decided to snooze after lunch but had woken up feeling thirsty. He was still somewhat groggy as he shuffled into the passage to reach the kitchen. That's when he saw Piotr.

Both men were stunned to see each other. Piotr made a dash past Dev towards the front door. Dev snapped out of his stupor and tripped Piotr as he moved past him. The back bag was flung down to the floor. Dev grabbed the fallen Piotr in a chokehold. Even though Piotr was a strong man he knew he had met his match.

Piotr struggled but was not able to free himself. Then things happened in a flash. Piotr noticed a heavy candle stand in the passage, he snatched the metal object and brought it crashing down on Dev's head. The blow knocked out Dev in an instant and he lay passive on the floor with blood oozing out of his wound. Piotr stood up and picked up his black bag, he peeked inside to see the laptop which looked undamaged. He slung the bag across his shoulder.

He was quite sure that the man lying in the passage was dead. He was still dazed by the turn of events, but he needed to think fast. He knew that leaving the chalet with a dead man was not an option since Igor had demanded a clean operation. He needed to create a diversion by making this look like a burglary gone wrong. Many of the expensive articles lying around looked too heavy or unwieldy to carry out.

Piotr looked through a few rooms before reaching the master bedroom used by Jai. He noticed a wooden armoire and upon opening it found a bunch of keys. By looking at the keys he knew that one of them was for a safe; but he would need to locate where the safe was. His years of experience came in handy as he slid the armoire to the side and found the small safe on the wall behind.

He opened the safe and discovered just one item lying inside - an expensive looking brooch. Piotr put the brooch in his pocket, and rushed out leaving the safe open. He reached the passage and glanced to see the man still sprawled on the floor. In a moment he opened the front door and clicked it shut behind him. Being a quiet Sunday afternoon – nobody had seen or heard anything. Hurriedly, Piotr moved to his car and once inside started on his way towards his home in Aclens.

Jai could have had a better afternoon. Though he had won the game 3 to 2, he was not happy dropping some of his serves and on his drive back to the chalet kept thinking what he could have done better.

At about 5 pm he pulled into the driveway and switched his thoughts to the evening ahead. He planned to take Dev out to one of his favorite bars in Montreux. He wondered when they would have the Suntory whiskey that Veer had sent over.

Jai opened the front door and having taken a few steps in the passage was stunned at the sight of Dev lying inert on the floor. He bent down and touched Dev and felt a faint pulse. He straightaway dialed the emergency number and then called Henri and Louise over the telecom.

The ambulance and police arrived very quickly with their lights flashing and sirens wailing. The medical team secured Dev's deep wound and gently lifted him onto the stretcher; within minutes the ambulance was on its way to the hospital.

Jai was informed that the investigating detective would arrive shortly. He did not want to wait for the detective and rushed off to the hospital to be with Dev.

Meanwhile, the police took photographs where Dev was found lying and dusted the place for fingerprints. The metal candle stand with evidence of blood was taken for analysis. They went over the property and checked each room one by one.

Upon entering Jai's bedroom, the police found the armoire to be out of place and the safe lay open with nothing inside. They called Jai to inform him about the safe. He instantly realized that the invaluable family jewel, *Soomjam*, had been stolen and he very briefly explained the value and significance of the family jewel to the police.

The news of the theft barely registered with Jai as he was worried about his brother. Dev had been wheeled into the emergency room where the doctors were operating on him. Jai was also overcome with guilt for having left Dev alone. The hospital staff was quite sympathetic, but apart from saying that Dev's skull had been fractured and that it looked like touch and go, no one shared anything further. Jai sat in the hospital lobby and anxiously waited for the doctors to give him some news.

As he waited, Jai called his sister Gauri in Antwerp. When she came on the line, Jai requested her to hold as he wanted to conference the line with Veer in India. When both were on the phone, Jai broke the alarming news of the assault on Dev and his critical condition to them. For several seconds there was complete silence as a sense of total disbelief enveloped them all.

Jai then went on to convey the theft of *Soomjam* to Gauri and Veer. "It looks like the robber was after the brooch and did not expect to find Dev in the house. I feel guilty for leaving him at home!"

Gauri could not maintain her composure, and tears streamed down her cheeks as she thought of poor Dev in his present condition. She had many fond memories playing with him and Jai at the Rangmahal palace in Dhawalpur. She remembered how they could never find Dev while playing hide and seek; he knew all the secret passageways and could hide for hours. Growing up, there was never a dull moment with Dev around.

Veer was very disheartened that a younger brother he loved dearly was now fighting for his life. Even though Dev was their step brother, none of them had ever felt that distinction. Veer being twelve years elder to Dev had always felt a father-like responsibility towards him. He somehow felt cheated by the circumstances.

Both Veer and Gauri felt concerned about Jai, knowing how close he was to Dev. They asked him if either ought to travel to Montreux. Jai told them to hold off till they had a better assessment on Dev's condition.

When she put the phone down, Gauri straightaway went looking for her husband Pranav to convey the news to him.

At his end, after finishing the call, Veer again dialed a number in the UK.

A little later, Jai received an update from the doctor. They had performed surgery on Dev's skull; he had however lost a lot of blood and had slipped into a coma. Luckily the blow was to the side of the head and missed hitting the brain directly. He was now fighting for his life and they would need to monitor his progress minute by minute. They promised to keep Jai informed and he returned to the chalet at around 8.30 pm.

Detective Jean-Philippe Basler had recently joined the investigation team at the police department in the Canton of Vaud. He was a smart looking man in his early forties; with an easy going demeanor. He had dark curly hair, highly intelligent eyes and an intense look. He was a determined man with the persistence of a hound. Basler started his police career eighteen years ago in Bern. For the last five years he had been assigned to the Swiss National Central Bureau for Interpol operations.

Before driving up to Jai Singh's home, the detective had made discreet enquiries about the Singh family. He had found out that Jai's grandfather was Maharaja Gaj Singh who ruled Dhawalpur till 1949. Like other kingdoms in India, the Dhawalpur monarchy was dissolved and acceded to the newly formed republic of India. The Maharaja retained his title and was given a privy purse. Both these entitlements were subsequently abolished in the 1970s.

Jai's father Jog Singh was born in 1945 and had been a foremost Polo player in his youth. Upon Gaj Singh's death in 1995, he became the titular Maharaja of Dhawalpur. Jog Singh had married two times. He and both his wives died in a plane crash in 2005 when their private aircraft crashed in the hills near Dhawalpur.

It appeared that the Singh family still retained formidable wealth and properties in India and abroad. The chalet was bought by Jai's grandfather in 1975 and was one of the prime properties in the Montreux area. Basler also knew that Jai was a famous scientist, as there were often articles about his research in the papers.

At about 9 pm, Basler was greeted at the door by Henri who showed the detective the spot in the passage where Dev was found and told him that Jai was in the study. The detective observed the scene of assault and noticed the blood patches on the floor and the carpet.

Basler found Jai looking quite stunned with the events of the evening and distressed about his step brother's condition. The detective expressed his sympathy and started by asking Jai about his whereabouts for the day and a few questions about Dev. "Mr. Singh, I know you are quite shaken up, but I would like to get some background and details about the event and also your own activities for the day", said Basler.

"Detective, Dev is my step brother; you see, my father married twice. Dev came to Switzerland yesterday from India and planned to spend a few days with me. We had a late breakfast around 11 am and I left home about 2 pm for my usual game of Sunday tennis at the

Wellington Club. Dev wanted to catch up on his sleep and decided to stay back at the chalet. I was at the club till about 4.30 pm and reached home at 5 pm. The door was locked and I used my key to enter. I entered the lobby and was going across to the study when I discovered Dev lying in a pool of blood in the passageway. I called the emergency number immediately."

Not one to leave anything to chance, the detective asked Jai if he thought that Dev may have anything to do with the theft of *Soomjam*. Jai was taken aback by this blunt question and in his view a bizarre suggestion, and answered, "Dev is very dear to me, and I have absolutely no doubt that he is not connected to this incident. We were the closest in age and grew up together, this is a man I can trust with my life. Also Dev has been doing well and has a very successful business."

In the study where they were talking, Basler noticed two antique guns mounted on the wall and also some other antiques and curios. He now switched his attention to the missing jewel. "What can you tell me about *Soomjam*?"

Jai replied that the jewel was in the family for over 150 years. In 1864, Maharaja Ummed Singh of Dhawalpur (Jai's great grandfather's grandfather) had been presented with the brooch by a British General in exchange for supporting the British army against the Ranas of Kedarnagar.

"Hmm, this is most impressive", says Basler. "What do you think is the value of the brooch?" he asked.

"It is valued at around twenty million dollars," replied Jai.

Basler raised his eyebrows hearing the value. "When was it last valued?"

"Late last year, it celebrated 150 years in the family. There was a valuation conducted which established its price. The event attracted some coverage in newspapers, TV and the web about the jewel and its history."

"For such an expensive item why was it not in a bank locker?" asked Basler.

Jai explained that a week ago his sister, Gauri and her husband, Pranav, had visited Montreux and wanted to showcase *Soomjam* to a circle of friends and acquaintances who had heard so much about the jewel in the media since last year. So Jai had it taken out of the bank locker and brought it home. The showing took place on June 7th at Jai's chalet. His plan was to put it back in the locker this week.

"Hmmm, so the location of the brooch was not public knowledge," commented Basler, "looks like only a select group of people knew of its whereabouts." He then requested Jai for a list of all the people who had attended the showing.

"It would also be helpful if you could give me a photograph of the brooch", requested Basler. Jai went to his desk and pulled out a recent photo of the jewel.

The brooch looked very elegant in the photo with the large blue sapphire surrounded by glittering diamonds. There was an inscription on the bottom of the photograph which read, "Maharaja Ummed Singh of Dhawalpur was presented this jewel by General Patrick Howarth, Commander of the 4th Battalion on 6th May, 1864 for his invaluable support in the battle of Rahatgarh against the Rana insurgency. The center stone of the brooch is a 55 ct flawless blue sapphire ringed by 12 flawless 5 ct diamonds. The rare and unique sapphire is from the Soomjam Valley mines in Kashmir and possesses velvety blue color and fine purity."

Basler also wanted to know if there had been any earlier attempts to steal the jewel. "Yes indeed," replied Jai, "there have been at least 3 attempts in the last 150 years – all unsuccessful. The last attempt was in 2004 a few months before I came to Switzerland from India. There was no arrest made, but I am sure the Dhawalpur police should have all the records, if you are interested."

Basler asked Jai about the household staff at the chalet. "There is Henri Berry who is my valet and his wife Louise who helps with the kitchen, they stay in a cottage on the grounds," replied Jai.

Since Basler wanted to speak with them right away, he asked Jai for the directions to the cottage. "I will speak with them and leave, but I will request you not to travel outside the area for some time till the initial investigations are complete," said Basler and headed out to the cottage.

Meantime, Piotr returned to his home in Aclens on the outskirts of Lausanne. On his 50 minute ride he was busy thinking how his plan to slip in and out with the data had gone completely awry. Originally, the plan was for him to deliver the data to Igor in Geneva the next day - June 15th. He now realized that as soon as Igor learned of the events at the chalet he would come after Piotr to cover his own tracks. The news of the incident may break anytime now.

It became increasingly clear to him, that disappearing from Switzerland was going to be his best bet at this time. He would lose the hundred thousand dollars but saving his life seemed the wiser option! And at least there was this expensive looking brooch which in itself maybe worth tens of thousands.

Upon reaching his home, as soon as Piotr parked his car, he rushed to his desk, took out his laptop from the black bag and switched it on. Fortunately, the laptop had survived the drop to the floor at the chalet. He searched the web for information on the jewel he had just stolen using keywords like Jai Singh, brooch and jewel. He was astonished to learn that the jewel in his possession was worth twenty million dollars! His face became flushed with excitement and his heart started to thump wildly.

Piotr knew that on his own he did not have the wherewithal to sell such as expensive item. He would need to get a go between or an intermediary involved. He was also aware that he would only get 20% to 30% of the full value of the item. He estimated that even if he was to get 20% that would translate to four million dollars; hence enough for him to retire!

Piotr went over to his fireplace and burnt all the photographs he had taken of Jai's chalet and the surrounding area. He quickly packed a few belongings, his laptop and the jewel and called his brother, Radoslaw. Losing no further time, he jumped into his car and started driving south headed towards Marseille, France.

Gauri was 35; she had her mother's beautiful eyes, a sharp straight nose and a kind hearted look. Her shiny black silky hair almost touched her knees. Pranav, her husband was 37, a tall shrewd man who stooped just a little. He looked like a man who got what he wanted.

They had been married in 2005 in Dhawalpur at a week-long lavish affair attended by many of the rich, famous and noble in India. Shortly after that they had moved to Antwerp where Pranav had set up his gems trading business.

Gauri took a keen interest in fine arts and sponsored art schools in Dhawalpur as well as in Antwerp. She was also a founding member of an organization called "Adra" that helped needy children across the globe.

After ten years of marriage and no children, their relationship was more of a détente than anything deeper. Gauri found happiness in her philanthropic work whereas Pranav seemed to care more about his business.

After Jai's call, Gauri found Pranav sitting on the terrace in their villa in Antwerp in the elegant Cogels – Osylei neighborhood. She conveyed the news to Pranav about Dev's precarious condition and the theft of *Soomjam*. Pranav looked visibly upset to hear all this.

After a few minutes Pranav told Gauri that he was going for a walk outside. Once he stepped out, Pranav called his business partner Gaston Collard. Gaston was travelling to Amsterdam for a business trip returning to Antwerp on June 15th evening. They agreed to meet on June 16th morning in their office in downtown Antwerp.

It was around 10.30 pm and the chalet was enveloped in silence. Jai was still in the study feeling low and sad. There was a soft knock on the door and Henri entered the room.

He was a gentle soul in his mid-fifties; reliable, straightforward and devoted to Jai. Henri's father had been hired by Jai's grandfather over forty years ago. The Berrys had been the chalet caretakers and groundskeepers since then. When Jai came to Switzerland in 2004 to study at EPFL, Henri also assumed the role of the valet. In all these years, there had been no untoward incident at the chalet.

Henri expressed his concern for Dev to Jai. He too was quite fond of Dev and had met him on multiple occasions. He enquired as to how Jai was doing and if he could get him something to eat or drink. Jai was in no mood as he had lost his appetite.

Henri proceeded to tell Jai that Detective Basler had been to the cottage and asked some questions about whether Louise or he had seen anyone on the property and also of their own whereabouts. "We told him that we did not see anyone come or go and that we had been at the cottage all afternoon from around 2 pm till 5 pm."

The detective had also enquired about *Soomjam* and they told him that they did not have much knowledge of the jewel, except that they knew it was expensive. And because of the showing a week ago were aware that it had been at the chalet for these last few days.

Jai nodded his head, thanked Henri and requested him to retire to the cottage and that he would take care of himself for the evening.

As Piotr drove to Marseille he was talking to his brother Radoslaw and had relayed the sequence of events leading to his decision to come to Marseille. He knew he could trust his brother and now needed his help.

Radoslaw was four years older than Piotr. He was a quiet man with a large prominent jaw which he kept rubbing every few minutes. With his gray hair swept back and deep thoughtful eyes he looked more like a poet than a gangster.

He had helped Piotr many times in the past and recognized that this time it was going to be very tricky especially with the Russians involved. "Piotr you cannot stay with me, they will find you here, and we need to find you a safer location. Let me talk to a few friends and find out where you should stay. We will also need to get you a new cell phone and hide your car – else they will locate where you are. Give me a few minutes and I will call you back."

After making a few enquiries, Radoslaw found a place where Piotr could hide for some time. He called him back and gave him an address. He told Piotr that he would meet him at that location.

Piotr drove nonstop but there was heavy traffic and he reached the outskirts of Marseille at around 11 pm. He parked in a street in the northern part of the city. He then walked a few blocks to the address that Radoslaw had given.

Piotr knocked on the door and his brother let him in. It was a run down and shabby building and the apartment itself was sparsely furnished. But the neighborhood was just right and would keep him unnoticed and safe.

"Rad, I appreciate your jumping in to help," said Piotr, "I was about to walk out of the chalet when things just went out of control as this guy walked in from nowhere and ruined everything."

"Piotr you certainly are in a big bind, but there is no point thinking about how all this happened. Let us focus on what needs to be done now. The Russians and police will both be looking for you. You will need to lie low. And this is the new cell phone you need to use," he said, handing him the phone.

With great excitement in his voice, Piotr said "Rad, let me show you the jewel I found. This thing will change our future forever!"

Radoslaw looked suitably impressed with *Soomjam*, the blue stone in the center was bigger than a large coin – he had never seen a gem that huge. "Twenty million dollars, wow! Things may not be so bad after all! I know a fence in the area, her name is Maria Lato, she is someone whom we can trust and who can manage to set up a deal. Of course we cannot hope to get more than 25% of the value." He rubbed his jaw with great enthusiasm.

Piotr had already figured that out. "That's fine, I am sure we can share the amount fairly between us," he said.

"Ok, give me your car keys, I will need to hide the car somewhere safe," said Radoslaw, "Also, the Russians will soon start following me, so for your own safety, we should not meet. I will call Maria and you can go and see her, I will let you know when and where."

Jai had a fitful night and woke up early. When he picked up "*24 heures*" and "Tribune de Genève" he could see that the media had already picked up the story. The news was carried in all the leading newspapers, TV and internet. The assault was being linked to the stolen jewel.

Jai could see a clutch of reporters outside the chalet hoping to get a word with him or perhaps anyone they could talk to.

He had already sent a message to his office in EPFL about the events and that he would take leave on Monday; also that he would work from home for the rest of the week.

Later in the day he received calls from his friends and people from his workplace expressing their shock and concern. Pierre Crochon his boss at EPFL and Nicole Binoche, his next in command for the *Solara* project and many other colleagues called to express their support.

Sophie called to say she would stop by at the hospital. Jai felt the need to see her in this troubling moment.

Sophie was bright, beautiful and always cheerful. She wore her gleaming black hair in a bouffant style that reminded Jai of actresses in 1950s. He would tease her that since she worked in advertising, they should use her as a model for shampoo or soap.

Jai and Sophie met outside Dev's room at the hospital. She was visibly shaken by the incident. They picked up coffee and sat together in the hospital café for quite some time. She comforted Jai and told him that Dev would pull through. "You know he is a tough guy, and he is getting the best medical attention."

"I hope so," said Jai, "you know before I headed out to the club, Dev asked about you and wanted for us to see more of each other," said Jai.

They both smiled. Sophie pecked him on the cheek and went back to her office in downtown Montreux.

Veer Singh sat in the expansive living room of Rangmahal Palace cleaning his pipe. His brow was furrowed as the news from Switzerland had concerned him greatly. Shera sat on the carpet and whimpered softly wanting to walk outside.

As head of the household, Veer felt responsible for the wellbeing of his family. It had been a peaceful and prosperous 10 years, but his mind flashed back a decade when his parents and step mother were killed in the air crash, He still had an uneasy feeling about the past events.

Veer clicked his fingers and signaled Shera to get up. As he stepped outside and walked past the fountain, he got a call from UK and a woman's voice came on the line. "Hello Veer, this is Stacy, please hold as Sir John would like to return your call." In a moment Sir John's booming voice came on the line, "Veer, I missed your call yesterday, how can I help?"

The next morning Piotr checked for messages on his previous cell phone which he had shut down on his brother's instruction. There had been multiple calls from Igor and the messages had grown progressively threatening.

Radoslaw called him to provide directions to Maria's place. He had already spoken with her to fix the meeting and given her some background information on the jewel.

Having lived in Marseille, Piotr knew his way about quite well. He used public transport to get to her place. On the way he was dreaming about what he would do with the money. He thought about moving to South or Central America under a different identity and buying a farm in some remote location.

Maria was a tall business like woman who wasted no time on pleasantries. She had already done some research on *Soomjam*. Moreover, the story of the theft was all over the morning news. However her reputation had been built on complete discretion.

In her line of business you had to be completely unconcerned about where an artifact had originated from. For her the important thing was peddling the item forward and moving the money through the right channels.

Piotr handed the jewel to Maria and she performed a thorough visual examination of the brooch. As she examined it her eyes narrowed. She then performed thermal conductivity and UV tests and the puzzled look on her face only intensified. Finally after looking over the item one more time she turned to Piotr and said, "This is a fake! The sapphire and the diamonds are all synthetic stones. This is not worth more than ten thousand dollars."

Piotr was utterly distraught – he looked as if he had been hit by a lightning bolt. "Are you sure?" he managed to say feebly.

Maria gave him a cold look – she had no time to sit and commiserate with him. She just put the item in Piotr's pocket and firmly steered him out of the door.

On the way back to the apartment, Piotr could not help but think how sour his luck had been. He had not made a penny on the data he stole from Jai's laptop, the jewel had turned out to be a fake, he had an assault or murder to contend with and was now on the run from Igor. He called Radoslaw and communicated the bad news.

Piotr reached the apartment and started to pace up and down the room thinking about his situation. The turn of events had left him completely shaken up.

Later around noon, his brother called him and said, "Piotr, how about the data you stole, if the Russians want it so bad, we can be sure that it may have value for other folks as well. Why not look into that?"

"That is good thinking man! I was too muddled up to look at it from that viewpoint," said Piotr excitedly, "let me do some research and I will call you later."

Piotr pulled out his laptop and started looking at the files he had copied from Jai's machine. He also searched the web about Jai Singh's professional work.

Igor heard about the assault and robbery and realized that there would be intense scrutiny on the case. He knew that if Piotr got caught, it would jeopardize his own position. He decided it was best to eliminate Piotr swiftly. But he still did not know if Piotr had been successful in stealing the laptop data. There was of course no mention of the data in any of the media coverage and reports.

He picked up his phone and called Piotr. But his phone was switched off and Igor reached his voicemail. He tried a few more times and became very frustrated when he realized that Piotr had most likely flown the coop.

No sooner had he reached this conclusion, Igor received a call from a furious Sergei – who demanded an update. He apprised Sergei of the situation. Both men knew that even though the incident at the chalet had complicated things, getting rid of Piotr would safeguard their own interests.

Igor lied to Sergei that he had already dispatched a team to find and eliminate Piotr. He assured Sergei that he would try to get the data if Piotr had been successful in stealing it from Jai's machine.

After keeping the phone down, Igor assembled two of his trusted henchmen and provided them a description of Piotr and his address in Aclens.

The two men arrived at Piotr's home and forced open the door. There was nobody in the house. The men set about going through Piotr's papers and personal items to find clues as to where he may have gone.

In their rush to find something useful, they knocked around furniture and other effects, removed items from shelves and emptied drawers. They looked under the mattress, carpet and every place possible in the small but messy apartment.

Finally, one of them got lucky. He found a piece of paper in an old file lying in a drawer that identified Piotr's brother Radoslaw Babicz. The paper had Radoslaw's past address in Marseille. Another paper in the file, a receipt, showed a past purchase Piotr had made in Marseille.

Happy to have found something of importance, they kept the file with them and walked out to their car. They had a brief conversation with Igor and got their orders from him to be on their way to Marseille without any delay.

Detective Basler was a man who could think quite clearly, but this case was confounding him. The intruder was a professional who had not left behind any clues. Enquiries in the neighborhood had not yielded any information. He did not quite know what to make of the case.

A very expensive jewel had gone missing, a man was nearly dead and there was simply nothing to go on. There were multiple open ended possibilities and he would need to evaluate the motivation and opportunities for all the scenarios.

Basler thought that from appearances and whatever he had seen thus far, Jai Singh seemed honest and could potentially be a genuine victim under the circumstances. But in his career he had also seen how looks could be deceiving. He could not in entirety rule out the possibility of insurance fraud. In such cases, the usual motive was money. He would need to investigate Jai's finances more closely.

Could the Berrys be suspected? While they lacked motive on the face of it, there could have been some hidden trigger point or it could be just plain greed.

Could the family in India have commissioned the theft? Was jealousy a motive?

And then there was the showing of the jewel last week. Could the sister, brother in law, office colleague or someone who attended the event be responsible?

Of course there was also the possibility of another party that had learned about the jewel. Some electrician, plumber, gardener, or someone random. But who?

With so many ideas jostling about in his mind, the detective started by finding out who Jai's accountant was, to learn more about the state of his finances.

He also gathered his investigation team and shared the list of people that had attended the showing of *Soomjam* at the chalet. He wanted each of them to be interrogated and their statements and whereabouts established for the day of the crime.

He also wanted his team to speak with Gauri and Pranav over the phone. He further instructed them to be on the lookout for any incident or activity in the local area that seemed suspicious.

Basler's investigations did not yield very much. Jai's finances appeared to be in good shape. He had no debts, a very sizeable bank balance, large assets both in Europe and in India and a highly paid job, so chances of him having committed fraud did not appear to be high, at least from a monetary perspective.

His team ran background checks on Gauri, Pranav and all the attendees of the event at Jai's chalet. They were also able to meet with or at the least speak to a number of them.

The few things they found which could seem somewhat suspicious were that Lady Tara had traveled to London a few days after the showing. Nicole had opened a bank locker the next day and one other attendee had made several trips to a jeweler in Geneva.

But overall, these appeared to be people in good public standing and on the face of it there was nothing untoward that could be ascertained.

Basler wanted his team to continue probing the background of the individuals just in case anything turned up.

Later that day his team received information of a house being broken into in the Aclens area. One of the neighbors had seen the damaged front door and had reported it to the local police. Basler was informed that the house belonged to someone by the name of Piotr Babicz who had been suspected of some local burglaries in the past but had never been convicted.

Basler decided to make a trip to Aclens and in 45 minutes was parked outside Piotr's home. He moved past the police tape and entered the house. Inside, he could see the signs of things being knocked about as if somebody had been looking for someone or something. Papers and household articles were lying strewn about.

In the fireplace, Basler saw what appeared to be some burnt photographs. Using a tweezer he gently picked up a partially burnt photograph in which he could faintly make out what looked like a boating dock. Could this be Jai's dock, wondered Basler.

He left the scene and on his way back to Montreux called his friends in Interpol and asked them to find out more about Piotr Babicz.

On the 16th morning Pranav sat down with Gaston, a man of rather large proportions with a scraggly beard. Upon seeing Pranav's ashen face, he asked "You look pale, what's the matter, mon ami?"

"You will not believe the news from Montreux. *Soomjam* has been stolen and my brother in law Dev has been assaulted!" replied Pranav. Both men fell silent for a few minutes.

Before joining Pranav in the gems trading business, Gaston had made certain losses on diamond investments. To recoup the losses, he had resorted to dealing in blood diamonds[1]. This was despite the very strict controls on trading in dirty diamonds; especially after the UN resolutions had been passed in 2002.

All diamonds were now required to have Kimberley Certification whereby they needed to be certified as coming from a non-conflict source. The only way Gaston could do this was by falsifying the papers.

Pranav had helped Gaston during this phase which then led to them becoming good friends and later business partners. Gaston felt beholden to Pranav for helping him. Later, as a junior partner in the business he went along with all of Pranav's decisions.

In the last few years their business had suffered a little, but it was nothing out of the ordinary. Then a few months ago, Pranav had come up with the idea of stealing *Soomjam*. Gaston was very surprised to hear of this strange idea.

He asked Pranav the rationale for stealing the jewel and whether it would be a wise decision considering the risks involved. However Pranav had convinced Gaston that the jewel would be their safety net in case they hit another rough patch in their business.

Pranav's plan was to replace *Soomjam*, at the appropriate time with a superbly crafted replica of the jewel that Gaston would help source. He had told Gaston that Jai being a very wealthy man, and *Soomjam* being a family heirloom with much history attached to it, Jai would never sell the brooch.

1. *Blood diamonds also known as conflict or war diamonds are those that have been mined in a war zone and are traded to finance conflicts and insurgencies*

Also, since the jewel had been valued about a year ago, there would not be an occasion for it to be valued anytime soon. Hence the replica would remain unnoticed for a very long time.

Gaston knew of a jeweler who would do the job based on details and photographs of *Soomjam* provided by Pranav. The jeweler had then crafted a very accurate replica of *Soomjam* which could have tricked anyone.

Last week, on June 7th when Pranav and Gauri had visited Montreux for the showing, Pranav had cleverly switched the jewel with the replica during the reception that followed the showing. He had then secretly carried the jewel back to Antwerp and kept it in his office safe.

Learning of the theft at the chalet, Pranav now felt frustrated that all his planning had gone askew. There were chances that the fake would get discovered for what it was and the spotlight might turn on him sooner or later. The thought of going to prison was not at all a pleasant notion.

Pranav leaned forward and said softly, "There is only one option, we have to eliminate Jai to prevent matters from getting out of hand."

Gaston was completely taken aback, "But he is your brother in law!" he cried.

"We don't have much choice," Pranav responded. "After the valuation last year, *Soomjam* had been sitting in the bank locker till the showing on June 7th. Once Jai learns that the jewel is a fake, he will be able to piece together that the switch between the real jewel and fake took place on the day of the showing."

"Yes, but what if Jai has already told the police about the showing in Montreux. Would that not cast suspicion on you in any case?" retorted Gaston.

"True, but there were several people at the showing and the jewel was passed around in the room, hence as far as the police is concerned I will be one among many suspects," said Pranav, "If we get rid of Jai and plant another fake on him, it will make the case quite murky. One option the police will need to evaluate is that Jai himself was involved in some underhand dealing or fraud."

Gaston nodded, "That should throw them off the track."

Pranav continued, "And with Jai out of the picture, the case will eventually turn cold and lose the attention of the police and public. Let us make it look like an accident."

It seemed to Gaston that Pranav had set his mind on getting rid of Jai. With a convincing looking accident they might be able to pull it off. He nodded and said, "Let me contact Alex Black in Paris to work on the Jai angle, I will also contact the same jeweler to get another replica made."

As he had planned, Jai had been attending to his work from home; this way he could also spend some time at the hospital and be with Dev. In the early hours of the morning it had rained quite a bit, but the rain had eased off by mid-day.

In the afternoon, it was still cloudy outside when Jai decided to visit the hospital and meet with the doctor in attendance. He was told that Dev was stable physically and the wound was starting to heal. But they could not be sure if and when he would come out of coma. This was not at all encouraging for Jai who had been hoping to hear better news.

When he was still at the hospital, Nicole from his office dropped in to meet Jai and enquire about Dev. Nicole was a brunette in her mid-thirties, a little plump and generally lively and cheerful. However, she seemed quite sad today and deeply concerned about Dev.

Jai told her that things were not very bright. She offered her support and told him to not lose hope. Sophie told Jai that she would keep visiting Dev in the hospital after work hours. She had met him on several occasions at the chalet and the two got along quite well.

When Jai returned home, Henri and Louise also paid a visit to the hospital. They were quite perturbed to see Dev in this condition. They sat in his room for quite some time hoping to catch any sign of improvement. It was not just Dev's state that was disturbing to them but also thinking about what Jai must be going through and how he would be coping with this grim situation.

Igor's men had reached Marseille on Monday evening and had checked into a hotel in a dubious looking neighborhood. It was a cheap glitzy place covered in Formica which was stained with age. The lobby had the smell of stale cigarette smoke wafting in the air; and the dimly lit corridors reeked of cheap perfume.

The next morning they met some of their Russian contacts in Marseille to get more information on Radoslaw. It was not very difficult and after a few phone calls, someone was able to track down his address.

Their plan was to observe Radoslaw's home and his movements leading up to Piotr.

Piotr had spent the previous day searching for information on the web and he had been quite productive. The next day, sitting in the apartment, sipping coffee with his laptop in front, he had learned sufficient details about Jai's work as a nuclear scientist and the *Solara* project. He realized that the information he had copied may very well be a gold mine in itself. In yet another twist of fate, things had started looking promising again!

He had been in the identity theft business and had dealt with buying and selling stolen personal data. This information trade typically happened on the "Dark Net", a part of the internet where parties remained anonymous and were able to deal in contraband and illegal goods and services.

Piotr frequently used an anonymous black market bazaar called *Evolution*. He would use the same marketplace and log in through Tor[2] to anonymize his communication. He set up the *Solara* offer on the marketplace with a simple message – "Nuclear fusion information on breakthrough project *Solara* available in exchange for half a million dollars to be paid in bitcoins". He also communicated in his message that he had in his possession 6 files in all, with one being a synopsis of the project.

He then poured himself another cup of coffee and settled down patiently waiting for fish to snap at the bait.

---

2.   *Tor (The Onion Router) is free software for enabling anonymous communication using encryption. This makes it difficult for anyone including authorities to track the user's web location and activities*

When he stepped into the office that morning, Detective Basler called the forensics department. He wanted to find out if there was any other additional information they had discovered based on the tests done on the candle stand. Also if there were any fingerprints that could help the case. So far there was no encouraging information. The thief seemed to have covered his tracks well.

Later that afternoon, he received a call back from the Interpol. His contacts had run a check on Piotr and found out that he had earlier operated with his brother in Marseille working for a Polish gang. When things became hot he had moved to Switzerland. His brother Radoslaw had relocated to Warsaw but had subsequently moved back to Marseille. In the last few years, Piotr had been known to operate as a cyber thief and a burglar specializing in data theft.

The information puzzled Basler, since it did not fit the profile of a burglar specializing in a jewel heist. But he knew that Piotr was somehow connected to the robbery at Jai's chalet. He walked over to his boss' office – police chief at the Canton of Vaud.

Basler conveyed to the chief the progress he had made and the possible connection of Piotr Babicz to the case. There was still a doubt in the chief's mind as the information on Piotr did not seem to fit the case; since for the last many years he had operated as a cybercriminal.

The first party to pick up the drift of the *Solara* offer was MI6 as part of their regular surveillance of the dark net. An analyst in London saw the information and compiled a report that included the following highlights.

Report urgency: Critical

Report category: Classified information for sale on dark net

Program: Solara – nuclear fusion project

Lab & location: EPFL, Switzerland

Countries involved in Solara: UK, Switzerland, France, Germany

Key people on the project: Pierre Crochon (Director), Jai Singh (Project Leader), Nicole Binoche (Assistant Project Leader)

Program status: Project breakthrough, results classified

The report was straightaway sent up to the leadership and reached the desk of Sir John Cleese - Deputy Chief of MI6 and Director of Operations. He was a short portly man with a handlebar moustache, a rather funny looking character. His demeanor did not betray the sharpness of his mind nor indeed the spy that he was.

Sir John knew of the *Solara* project and its strategic importance to the four countries in partnership on this initiative. Through Veer Singh he had independently learned of the incident at Jai's chalet in Montreux even before the news had spread through media. He was quick to connect the dots.

Sir John established contact with the head of the Swiss Federal Intelligence Service (FIS) based in Bern Switzerland. He told his Swiss counterpart of the data theft and the attempt to sell it on the dark net.

Both men discussed the measures that the Swiss authorities and police would need to take to apprehend the criminal and secure the information. They understood the urgency of stopping it from being sold on the web.

43

They also discussed the possibility for their agencies to bring down the web marketplace where the project was up for sale. However, they also knew that this could well be futile as information could then be put up on other marketplaces.

As soon as they finished the call, the FIS head connected with the police chief in the Canton of Vaud.

Around the time that the *Solara* information was noticed by MI6, it was also noticed by FSB. Since the *Solara* project was being handled by Sergei Zhuk, the report came to him. It was a dark grim day in Moscow and Sergei's mood was no better. The chain of events had completely spiraled out of control. Not only did Sergei not have the *Solara* information, it was now up for sale on the dark net!

It was ironic that Leonid Batcheff decided to call Sergei just then, wanting to know if there was any progress on the *Solara* information. Sergei barked as he told him that his team was working on it and he would have an update shortly.

His phone call to Igor was brief, "You bumbling idiot! Make sure you find Piotr before anyone else has a chance to buy the information."

Igor desperately called his men in Marseille and they told him that despite their enquiries they had been unable to locate Piotr so far. They had traced where Radoslaw lived, but Piotr was not staying there. They were also following Radoslaw to see where he went – but so far there was no sign of Piotr.

Igor commanded, "Then bring in Radoslaw and extract the information from him – he will know where Piotr is."

When the phone rang in the office of the police chief of Canton of Vaud he was sitting with Basler. He gripped the phone tightly hearing what the FIS head conveyed to him.

After his conversation, the chief turned to Basler and said "You are right, Piotr is your man. It looks like the break in was for a sensitive nuclear fusion project at the EPFL called *Solara*. Jai Singh is the project leader. Attempts are being made to sell the project information on the dark net."

Listening to this, all the pieces seemed to click into place. Basler said, "I have a strong feeling that Piotr has skipped to Marseille and I would like to go there immediately. There is no time to lose."

The chief nodded, "I agree and the French police will extend full cooperation, they are also partners in the *Solara* project. I will call my contacts right away."

Both men agreed that an Interpol alert should be issued for Piotr.

Basler called his team and apprised them of the latest developments. The focus of their enquiry would need to change. He told them that Piotr would likely have acted on behalf of some third party and it was important to start thinking in that direction. In light of this, Basler wanted security to be provided to Jai Singh for the foreseeable future.

Basler then called Jai and requested for an emergency meeting between himself, Jai and Pierre Crochon the director at EPFL about the theft of data.

Jai agreed to coordinate with his boss. He was able to reach Pierre who understood the urgency and consented to meet at short notice. They decided to meet at the police station in Montreux.

Once the three were together in the room, Basler conveyed to them a gist of what had transpired. Both Jai and Pierre were quite astounded to learn about the data theft.

Pierre was a tall, good-looking man with brown eyes and gray hair swept back. "This news is making me extremely nervous and the situation itself is very treacherous for us," he said, "Jai and the team have spent years toiling on this venture and national interests of four countries are tied to this project."

Basler pointed out, "Well, it seems that the solicitation for the data was put up today. It may be a few days before any transaction can actually take place," he continued, "Of course the fact that the data is out there is of great concern. We have reason to believe that the thief is an Aclens resident called Piotr Babicz who has likely crossed the border and is in Marseille. I myself am leaving for Marseille today evening to meet with the local police there."

Jai and Pierre wanted to know how Basler had zeroed in on Piotr and his current location. He said, "This is still circumstantial but Piotr is a cybercriminal who deals in technology, data and identity theft. Also, I did find a partially burnt photo in his Aclens house that shows what could be the dock outside Jai's chalet. There is no one at that house now. His brother is based in Marseille, which was also Piotr's earlier base, so we think he is there now."

Both of them nodded. Basler went on to say "I am sure you will inform your team to be extra cautious with their data and implement all needed precautionary measures. Also, I am providing security to Jai – just to be on the safe side."

Pierre and Jai agreed that this was the best course of action. They wished Basler luck in his mission in Marseille.

On his way back to the chalet, Jai stopped by at the hospital to check on Dev. There was not much improvement, and Dev lay there with multiple leads and monitors attached; observing him for any signs of progress. Jai sat next to him for some time feeling hopeless and distressed.

As he drove home, Jai called Sophie to tell her about the latest developments. "So you mean that the intruder, supposedly this fellow, Piotr, was basically after the data on your computer?"

"That's what it is looking like now," said Jai, "and the big worry is that he is trying to sell the information on the internet. The detective believes he is in Marseille and is going over there to coordinate with the local police."

"Jai, I am sure they will catch him soon," said Sophie, "Tomorrow I am going to Geneva but I want to visit Dev on the 19th which is Friday; if you are free sometime that day we can meet at the hospital." Jai agreed.

As Jai arrived at the gates of his chalet, he could see a police car already parked in the driveway. It seemed like Basler was taking the security bit quite seriously.

Radoslaw had worked the streets long enough to know that he was being followed. He had already made sure that he would not go anywhere near Piotr. He also knew that the Russians would accost him soon to try and learn about Piotr's whereabouts.

When evening descended upon Marseille, Radoslaw decided to slip away under the cover of darkness. He packed a small bag and sneaked out into the street from the back door. He used multiple modes of transport and made sure that he was not followed.

Finally he reached an unused warehouse that he had used for his operations in the past. This area of town was part residential and part industrial. If he needed to, he could stay here and remain unnoticed for a long time. Once things had cooled a bit, he could even let Piotr move in here. But for now it was better and safer to stay separate.

Meanwhile, Piotr had received two anonymous messages via *Tor* for the dark net transaction. The parties sounded interested and both wanted to see the entire data. They were not willing to risk paying a large sum of money without verifying the content first.

Unknown to Piotr, of the parties that had contacted him, one was MI6 and the other was FSB. Their motivations were different. While MI6 wanted to keep a tab on Piotr, it had neither the intent nor the need to actually buy the information.

On the other hand, FSB was keeping its options open. If Igor's men were successful in tracking down Piotr, FSB would be able to grab the information for themselves, and stem the competition, if any. The added bonus being that they would not need to pay anything. If Igor's men were unsuccessful, then the alternative would be to transact through the dark net and pay the half million dollars being demanded.

Piotr responded to the messages by saying that while he had tangible information he would not be willing to reveal the entire data without being paid first. To build confidence, he sent over the *Solara* synopsis from the information that he already had.

Igor's men waited for darkness to fall before making their way into Radoslaw's apartment. They broke the lock and entered inside. They looked around the entire place, but to their surprise and disillusionment, there was no one inside.

They decided to wait for Radoslaw at the apartment, believing he would turn up sooner or later. They saw his bottle of vodka lying on the countertop and settled down for the long night ahead.

It was about an hour later that three men entered the apartment and after a brief struggle managed to overpower Igor's men. After disarming them and removing their phones, they tied their hands and put hoods over their heads. They bundled them into a van waiting outside.

Igor's men were driven to a location outside Marseille and hustled into a decrepit looking basement. There were armed men outside to make sure that they stayed put.

The leader of the three then called Radoslaw to indicate that the job had been done. Radoslaw's plan was to establish a negotiation – his and his brother's life for the life of the two men he had captured. The three men who did the job were members of the gang he now operated; like him, they were all Polish and ex members of the South Side Gang.

There was no direct flight from Geneva to Marseille, so it was late on Wednesday that Basler checked into a hotel on the Corniche du Président J.F. Kennedy in Marseille. He loved the town and this area provided magnificent views of the Mediterranean and Prado Beaches.

The next morning he was up early and while having his breakfast, took in the view of the sea from his room. However, his mind was occupied with finding Piotr. He planned to meet with his contact from French Interpol who was now a detective with the Marseille police.

At 10 am he dressed and set out for his meeting which would take place in the detective's office on La Canebière not far from the Vieux Port area. He took a taxi and reached the police station in a few minutes.

Josiane Dhéry was waiting for him in her office. She was of medium build with green eyes and exuded an air of relaxed competence. Basler had known Josiane for many years from the days when she was with the French Interpol.

They had worked on several cases and had met each other on many occasions, both in France as well as in Switzerland. She had grayed in these years – but her smile was still very wide. The two greeted each other warmly, exchanged a few pleasantries and sat down to discuss the business at hand.

Basler proceeded to give Josiane an update on the case. In passing, she had already heard about the assault and robbery in Montreux. Her interest was heightened when Basler talked about Project *Solara* and its strategic importance to France, Switzerland, UK and Germany.

He concluded by saying that he had good reason to believe that Piotr may have crossed over to Marseille and gave her the rationale for his thinking. He also told her that an Interpol alert would have been issued by now. She agreed that Marseille was a possible location for Piotr to be in.

Basler looked hard at Dhéry and he sounded earnest when he said, "Josiane, this case is just too important and I need you to be personally involved."

"Don't worry Jean-Philippe," said Dhéry, "You have brought me an interesting case. Feels like old times!"

Basler looked somewhat relieved, "Also we need to locate Piotr with great speed. I know Marseille is a big city and this is not easy. Where will you start?" he asked.

"Radoslaw must be helping his brother, we will first try to find him and that will lead us to Piotr," said Dhéry, "Also, I have a feeling that Piotr may be in the northern part of town so we will focus our efforts there. We will also circulate a description and photograph of him at all the local police stations."

Basler said, "This sounds logical, but on the Radoslaw angle, my hunch is that he himself would have disappeared by now."

"That's a strong possibility, but I think we may know some of his associates and if we round up a few, it will put the right pressure on him."

"Could you also start monitoring his cell phone? Maybe that will help as well." requested Basler.

For the time being, Basler felt he had partly achieved what he had come to Marseille for. He would stay back in the city one more day just in case there was a lucky break. If not, he planned to leave for Switzerland the next day, by afternoon.

Basler thanked Dhéry and having said his goodbye he caught a taxi to the Vieux Port area from where he planned to stroll back to the hotel.

When Igor called his men that day he was expecting progress. What he got was someone on the line claiming that his men had been captured! "Ok here's the deal," said Radoslaw rubbing his jaw, "you lay off me and my brother and I will let your men live. If you send more men – we can start a turf war but it will cost us both. Suggest we leave it here."

Igor knew that the situation looked bleak, and he did not have too many options. He said, "How do I know my men are alive?"

"You don't, but you will need to take my word," countered Radoslaw and cut the phone.

With the situation becoming the way it was, Igor knew that there was no longer any merit in knocking Piotr out of the equation. What he had hoped to achieve was his silence, but now what he would get if he went after him and his brother would be more publicity.

With great trepidation he called Sergei to let him know of the situation.

When he received Igor's call, Sergei was livid. Nothing seemed to have worked as per plan and now Igor's men were captured by those who should have been on the run! The more he had engaged with Igor, the more ridiculous the situation had become. Sergei decided that he would deal with Igor later.

Sergei had already started working on the counter plan. His bargaining position had become weak and he was willing to pay the half million dollars now being demanded by Piotr; but he needed to make sure that the data was genuine. After all, this was an anonymous transaction on the *Evolution* marketplace. He had therefore sent the synopsis that had been uploaded by Piotr to Leonid Batcheff for analysis.

Sergei then called Leonid. "Well, have you looked at the data?" asked Sergei.

"I have been away from Moscow and have not reviewed the information yet. I will be back on Sunday evening and will give you an answer by Monday."

"The more you delay, the longer it will take to set up the deal. I can only get into the deal once I know that the information looks real. No later than Monday then," barked Sergei.

Alex Black's flight to Charles de Gaulle landed on time. After receiving Gaston's message; he had cut short his vacation in Greece where he was rock climbing on the Kalymnos islands with his girlfriend. He was a muscular man of medium height with cold eyes and a calculating look. He picked up his black Range Rover from the airport parking and headed home.

His apartment in the Montparnasse neighborhood was not far from the entrance to the Catacombs of Paris. The apartment itself was sparsely furnished in shades of white and gray reflecting the icy personality of the owner.

He sent an encrypted message to Gaston to get additional details of the contract in Montreux, "Tell me about the job."

"Your mark is a chap called Jai Singh, he works at the EPFL and lives in Montreux. You will get 500K when the job is done. Needs to happen fast and needs to look like an accident."

"If it needs to look like an accident, I need to have some information on his movements and travel plans. In fact, if he goes out of town that would be ideal," said Alex.

"I will see what I can find," responded Gaston, "Also, I have sent you an artificial jewel that you will need to plant on the target when you do the job."

Alex opened up a browser and in a few minutes was able to get a generous amount of information on the target, his chalet in Montreux and the car he drove. He also learned that Jai had been in the news quite a bit in the recent past. It appeared that there had been an assault and a robbery at his chalet only in the past week. Once he got further information from Gaston on Jai's specific movements, he would work out his detailed plan.

Gaston called Pranav and told him that Alex Black was back in Paris and would soon mobilize to Switzerland to take care of Jai. However, Alex would need details on Jai's movements so that he could plan the hit with precision. Earlier in the day, he had dispatched the fake jewel to him using a circuitous multi-country route.

Pranav walked over to the living room where Gauri was putting some fresh cut flowers into a vase. "Gauri what is the news from Montreux? I hope Dev is doing better, have you spoken with Jai?"

"The last I spoke with Jai, things were still the same. Dev's condition has not improved and he is being monitored continuously. On the investigation, I understand that the thief has crossed the border and is now in Marseille."

"Oh, that's good so they are close to catching him," said Pranav hiding his concern. His heart beat faster as he thought about the truth behind the jewel being discovered.

"You know, poor Jai is stuck with all this happening around him. Wonder if he is still planning to go to Zermatt next week as he had mentioned during our visit," Pranav probed, "it will certainly be a change for him."

"I do think that is a good idea, if he could go just for a couple days," concurred Gauri. "I will talk to him and encourage him, he does need a break."

Though it was a beautiful sunny morning, Jai did not feel all that bright. He had been waiting to hear some cheerful news from the hospital, but there was nothing so far. After a light breakfast he headed over to the hospital where Sophie would be meeting him later in the day. The police security dutifully followed him there.

He sat on the chair next to Dev's bed. He was still grappling with how something like this could have happened.

Around lunch time, Sophie walked into the room and sat next to him. She was worried to see no improvement in Dev's condition and Jai too looked very drawn and stressed. "Have you any news from the detective?" she asked.

Jai responded, "Nothing from Marseille yet. I hope Basler has been able to make progress. It makes me very nervous that the data is out there; heaven forbid if it ends up getting sold."

Sophie put her arms around him, "Don't worry, I am sure it will all get sorted out."

Jai looked at her and tried to smile.

"Did you see that?" she asked suddenly. She thought she saw Dev's right hand move just a fraction. Jai shook his head, he had not noticed anything.

For a minute both glued their eyes in that direction. "You probably thought you did," said Jai. And then he saw it too, indeed Dev's right hand had shown a flicker of a tiny movement.

"Call the doctor, the nurse, do something!" Sophie was beside herself with excitement.

Jai ran out into the corridor and found a nurse who promptly called the doctor in attendance. By now Dev's hand movement had become a bit more perceptible.

Looking at the EEG data, the doctor was able to see heightened brain activity, which was a sign of progress but he could still not predict how things would go. Even this was welcome news for Jai and Sophie.

Josiane Dhéry had already assembled a team the day before and provided instructions about Piotr. The news had been circulated widely and the word was out on the street that the police were sparing no effort to track down Piotr.

Just to get the message across very clearly, Dhéry rounded up a few of Radoslaw's associates. She was able to get his cell phone number and started monitoring his calls. Later that day, Radoslaw decided that the current status quo could not be maintained for long. He called his brother.

"Piotr, the police is looking for you all over with a fine toothcomb. There is an Interpol alert as well. It will be impossible to get you across any border."

"Is it all that grim Rad?"

"They have already rounded up a few of my men. And the way things are, they will find you in a matter of days if not hours. I am told they are already focusing on the north part of the town."

"What are you suggesting then?"

"Look, I have saved you from the Russians. But I think it is better to strike a deal with the police. After all they will not kill you," said Radoslaw rubbing his jaw.

"What do you mean deal?"

"Well, it will be like a surrender and they will need to treat you nice. Also, the news says that the guy you assaulted is doing better, so you will only get charged with robbery and assault, not murder."

Piotr had no better plan or argument and they decided that Radoslaw's idea was the best under the circumstances.

"Before I call the police, why don't you make a copy of the *Solara* data – maybe I can work on selling it and we can square up later," Radoslaw offered. This made sense to Piotr.

Even before Radoslaw could give the signal to the police, they had already zeroed in on Piotr's location by triangulating the cell phone signal. The status was communicated to Dhéry and she called Basler.

In less than 5 minutes, the police were at Piotr's door. He was taken into custody as was his laptop and the fake jewel. He did not get a chance to copy the data as suggested by Radoslaw.

Basler and Dhéry were waiting in her office on La Canebière for Piotr to be brought in. He was taken to an interrogation room where they questioned him on the *Solara* data for sale on the dark net. Piotr told them that he had not made any transaction other than sharing the synopsis file. That sounded plausible, but it was something that Basler would need to validate soon.

Basler asked Piotr, "Mr. Babicz, we need to know who contracted you for the *Solara* information?"

At first Piotr was reticent to provide this information, but realized that the more he cooperated with the police, the better would be his chances to secure a lenient punishment. He told Basler, "It was the Russians, I was contracted by Igor Primakov."

Basler pressed more, "Can you substantiate this further?"

"I have cell phone records, moreover the Russians have come to Marseille looking for me."

Basler and Dhéry left the interrogation room. Piotr had not yet revealed to them that the jewel he had stolen had proven to be a fake.

Basler looked at Dhéry and said, "Josiane, you know I couldn't have hoped for a better outcome, this is all thanks to you. I have one other request, I don't want the news of Piotr's capture to go out or for the media to report anything yet. Could you please have your folks keep a tight lid on this? There are many loose ends to tie up first."

Dhéry assured him of her cooperation on this. She also helped expedite Piotr's extradition and the next morning, Basler and Piotr were on the flight to Switzerland.

Sir John received a call from the head of FIS telling him that Piotr had been caught in Marseille. His laptop had been secured, and as per Piotr the dark net transaction had not yet happened. But the team was still working to validate whether Piotr had shared any critical information with other parties.

Earlier, MI6 had already sent over the *Solara* synopsis file they had received from Piotr for analysis. It was found to contain only the project overview but no details.

Sir John was also told that the job seemed to have been contracted out by the Russians, something he had suspected all along. Both men were satisfied with the progress the case had made. Sir John conveyed his compliments to the team that had worked on the case.

Before putting down the phone they agreed that as a matter of national security they would continue to probe further; to learn more about the parties that were trying to transact with Piotr on the dark net.

A few hours after Piotr's capture by the police, Radoslaw was still at his hideout. He knew that the police were aware of his location, and he was playing it safe in case Igor had changed his mind.

As he was biding his time, he decided to call Detective Dhéry, "Hello Detective, this is Radoslaw. Your team was listening in so you know that I gave some good advice to my brother to hand himself in."

"That's true Radoslaw, but I am sure you have not called just to earn brownie points."

"Well that too, but I do feel guilty at not being able to help my brother some more, so I was hoping that you can put in a word that they show him leniency."

"In that case what can you tell me about the Russian involvement? Piotr has told us that Igor was after him."

"Detective, I actually have two of Igor's boys in a basement under the care of my men. In case you need hard evidence of Russian involvement I can turn them over to you. I was keeping them as a tradeoff. My only promise to Igor was that I would not hurt them as long as they did not hurt us."

Dhéry smiled and said, "Let them be your guests for some more time. We have decided to keep the news of Piotr's capture under the wraps, so it may be a good idea for you to maintain status quo for a few more days."

She conveyed the news to Basler that the Russian involvement seemed to be a certainty.

It was on their flight from Marseille to Geneva via Paris that Piotr spoke of the jewel to Basler. "What do you mean *Soomjam* is a fake?" Basler was incredulous.

"I was planning on selling it and showed it to a fence who knows quite a bit about gems. Upon evaluation it was found that the diamonds and the sapphire are machine made synthetic stones," replied Piotr.

Basler would not believe that the jewel was a fake. But the serious look on Piotr face cast some doubt in his mind. This provided another strange twist to the events. Was burglary of the two items a coincidence or was it preplanned? Was Jai somehow involved in the murky affair? These and many other thoughts crossed Basler's mind.

When they reached Montreux, Basler decided to keep Piotr in a safe house. He did not want the news of his capture to be publicly released. He continued to be bothered by many unanswered questions as to who was behind all this.

It was drizzling outside when Jai received a call from the hospital in the morning. They told him that Dev was still feeling muzzy but was now conscious and had started uttering a few words. Filled with joy and with a wide smile, he rushed over to Henri and Louise, giving them the good news on his way to the garage.

Once he was on his way, he called Gauri and Veer to convey the delightful news. Gauri had a million questions and Jai promised to give her more details after his visit to the hospital.

He also called Sophie and Nicole who were very excited to learn of this wonderful development. Sophie promised to meet him at the hospital.

When he entered the room, Dev could still not move, but his eyes looked up and with some effort he could feebly say "Jai." That was enough to bring tears to Jai's eyes and he gently held his brother's hand.

"Don't talk – all that will come later. Take it easy for now."

Sophie entered the room and she welled up seeing Dev awake and Jai looking ever so happy.

Jai checked with the doctor who told him that Dev's recovery was looking quite promising but his physical recovery could still take several days or weeks for that matter.

Jai then got a call from Basler who was at the police station and wanted to meet him at the earliest. Jai told him that he was at the hospital but could be there in a few minutes. He left the hospital with Sophie giving company to Dev.

Basler met him at the door. "Would you like some coffee Mr. Singh?"

Jai replied that he would not mind a cup. Both men picked up their coffees from the office machine and walked over to Basler's office.

"Mr. Singh, we have apprehended the criminal. In fact, he in a safe house in Montreux as we speak. We believe that no dark net transaction has taken place, but we still need to confirm that."

"Congratulations Detective! That means you did a marvelous job in Marseille," said Jai, looking somewhat relieved.

Basler smiled and said, "Actually I was lucky and fortunate to find dear Josiane in Marseille. She is a detective with the Marseille police. We know each other from our Interpol days. She worked her magic on the streets and pressed the right buttons."

"I am glad that this got wrapped up rather quickly. What about *Soomjam*? Did you find it on him?"

Basler stared hard at Jai and said, "This is going to be a shock for you," and he paused there.

Jai looked at him apprehensively, as Basler took out the jewel from his bag and laid it on the table.

"Piotr says it is a fake! What can you tell me about that?" Basler's tone had hardened a little.

Jai's brow furrowed as he picked up the jewel and examined it closely. A look of disbelief came over his eyes and he moved it closer to the lamp on Basler's desk. "You are right, it is a fake!" he could barely whisper. "But we had the genuine one at the showing, I am positive about it!" he exclaimed. Surprise and disappointment were writ large on his face.

Just by looking at Jai, Basler knew that he was genuinely surprised and disappointed with this development. The notions he had entertained earlier about Jai's complicity began to evaporate.

Basler asked, "Mr. Singh, how are you able to tell it is a fake?"

"Detective, though it's a good copy, when I look at it closely, the stones themselves don't shine as bright as they do in *Soomjam*. And in the real brooch one of the diamonds is set at an angle which is very slightly different from the other eleven diamonds. My dad had showed me this detail many years ago."

Jai continued, "Looks like somebody switched the real with the fake at the time of the showing!"

"How can you be sure?" asked Basler.

"After I fetched *Soomjam* from the bank locker I was sitting with Gauri and we got talking about its history and its unique features. I actually showed her the diamond which is set differently."

"So Gauri can corroborate the discussion you had. Was there anyone else there when you showed her this feature?"

Jai shook his head, "No, it was after dinner, it was just the two of us. After that I put *Soomjam* back in the locker in my room and the locker keys were always with me."

Jai continued to ask a question, "Do you think it is at all likely that Piotr himself could have replaced *Soomjam* with the fake?"

"We cannot completely exclude the possibility, but it is highly unlikely. A jewel robbery does not fit his profile. Also, we already know that he had a contract to steal the data. Then the question arises did he plan to steal the jewel after he got the Russian contract?"

Basler continued to answer his own question, "Well in that case how would he even have known that the jewel was at the chalet and not in the bank locker as it usually is. My belief is that he stole the item to create a diversion as he claims, when he stumbled upon Dev whom he was not expecting to be in the house".

Jai agreed, "Yes, it is unlikely that Piotr is the 'real' *Soomjam* thief."

"So now we have to find the real thief behind *Soomjam!*" exclaimed Basler.

Basler wanted to clarify something and asked, "But tell me something Mr. Singh, how could someone get such a good replica created that even you did not realize that it was fake till you examined it closely today?"

"Detective, as you are aware it is a famous jewel after all and so its description and photographs are in the public domain. In fact there are books and encyclopedias that cover the subject of famous gems," said Jai.

Basler thought for a moment and said, "Let us not reveal that we know about its authenticity. In fact, we will make it public that the jewel has been irretrievably lost."

Jai gave him a puzzled look, "How will all this help?"

"We will put the thief's mind at rest and plan a trap. The thief is very likely someone who was present at the showing. This is where it will be useful to inject some drama into the whole thing," said Basler his eyes twinkling with mischief. "We will spread the word that the jewel was dropped into the Mediterranean while chasing the criminal at sea. We will also say that the chase was futile and he escaped."

Jai looked at him quizzically again, "I get the part about the jewel dropping into the sea. But why say that Piotr has escaped?"

"You see that has to do with *Solara*. We still need to find out more about the parties that were looking to buy the data. With news of Piotr's escape we can keep the interest of these parties alive on the dark net for some time. They will think they are continuing to deal with Piotr."

"Yes, that makes sense," agreed Jai.

"As for the deal that Piotr was trying to set up on the dark net, we believe that nothing has happened but as I said earlier, we do need to make sure that no important information was divulged to any party. We are trying to get Piotr to share his *Evolution* marketplace log in so we can actually get to know the exact status on the transaction. He has not cooperated so far."

"I hope that you can learn this soon, so we can rest easy on this matter." Jai continued, "Has Piotr revealed who was behind the contract of the data theft?"

Basler nodded, "Piotr says it was the Russians. An operator in Geneva, fellow called Igor Primakov."

Jai's eyes widened. He remembered his visit to Moscow about a month ago. He mentioned this to Basler who nodded. "Yes, it's possible that this was initiated after your visit."

"I have an idea," said Jai. But first I will need to discuss with Pierre. If he approves, we can meet on Monday, June 22nd to discuss."

As they wrapped up the meeting, Basler said "I would like to keep the fake and have some tests done if you don't mind."

"By all means," said Jai and Basler kept the fake jewel in his bag.

Basler called the lead investigator of his team and told her to spread the word in the media that the jewel was lost at sea. He also asked her to have the team refocus efforts on all the attendees of the showing.

On his way back to the chalet, Jai called Gauri to convey more details as he had promised. The splendid news about Dev having spoken to Jai, even though it was just one word was welcome news. She was overjoyed to hear that Dev was on a path of recovery. She had been praying hard every day and it seemed that her prayers had been answered.

"Jai, I would like to come down to Montreux next Friday and be with Dev. I will be there for a week and it will give you some relief as well. In fact while I am there, why don't you go ahead with your Zermatt plan as you had mentioned two weeks ago?"

What she said made sense, "Thanks much Gauri. It would be wonderful to have you here. Regarding Zermatt, let me check my schedule and I will confirm to you in a day or two."

"And the following weekend is your birthday, we can celebrate it together. I will also ask Pranav to join us."

Jai knew that he could trust Gauri and told her that the jewel that was recovered was a fake. "Gauri, the detective suspects everyone that attended the showing two weeks ago."

"Well that makes me a suspect too!" joked Gauri.

"You know that I have full faith in you. Why do you suppose I am telling you all this? Basler wants it to be known that the jewel was lost in the sea during Piotr's capture." Jai then explained the rationale behind Basler's thinking.

Gauri couldn't help herself, her mood had been uplifted with Dev's news, "Jai, if dad were alive, you know what he would have done to catch the thief?"

"What's that?"

"He would have called his favorite astrologer and had it all figured out!" They both chuckled at the thought.

"Anyway I get your point. This is what I am going to tell Pranav."

Gauri found Pranav in the study watching TV. "Pranav, I have some fantastic news! Dev is recovering, he is starting to talk!"

"That's great to hear! Hope he makes speedy progress."

"I have been praying for that. I will go to Montreux next Friday to be with him. In fact, I have suggested to Jai that he should head out to Zermatt while I am there."

This was music to Pranav's ears. "That's a great idea Gauri."

"After a week you can join me in Montreux, we can celebrate Jai's birthday on July 4th," suggested Gauri.

"That will work quite well," agreed Pranav.

"Well the other news is quite disappointing. Looks like the *Soomjam* fell into the Mediterranean as there was a boat chase in Marseille to catch the thief. They can't seem to recover it, waters are too deep."

"This is most disturbing!" said Pranav. Inside what he felt was pure elation, he could not have hoped for anything better.

When he knew that Gauri was busy, Pranav sidled out and called Gaston. "My friend, I have some wonderful news! Looks like the fake jewel has fallen into the sea while chasing the thief and they can't find it!"

"That's awesome! What do you want to do with Alex's contract on Jai?" asked Gaston.

"We will move forward on the contract," replied Pranav, "Who knows if they find the damn thing. In fact, it is possible that Jai may travel to Zermatt next weekend. It may be the perfect opportunity for Alex. I will confirm soon."

"And what about the second fake we sent Alex?" asked Gaston.

"Now that the first has fallen into the sea, we will not need to use the second, please ask Alex to get rid of it," responded Pranav.

Early Sunday morning, Basler came around to the safe house as Piotr was sitting on a chair contemplating his life in jail. He had done small stints earlier but nothing over 6 months. Life would not be easy at all if he had to spend years inside a cell.

Basler pulled up a chair and sat close by. "Piotr, I will come straight to the point. Once you are sentenced, depending on the prosecution's case you will get between 5 to 10 years in jail. If you continue to cooperate with me, I can work to minimize jail time."

"What do you need Detective?"

"We need to be sure about the dark net transaction."

"I already told you, I put up the details on Wednesday, June 17th and before anything could happen, you folks got to me by Friday."

"One way that we can be sure is if you share your *Evolution* account and password details."

Thinking of his life behind bars, Piotr decided he had nothing to lose. He figured that by the time he would get released from jail, the *Evolution* marketplace may no longer be in existence. In fact the technology itself would change considerably by then.

His only reluctance in sharing his account and password was that Basler would also get access to his other past shady deals. He confronted Basler about this issue who assured him that the police would only use it for the *Solara* transaction and not dig into his past deals.

That satisfied Piotr, "Do you have a pen and paper?" he asked.

"That's a good start Piotr," said Basler noting down the details. "And I will do what I can from my side."

As he walked out, Basler thought that this had been easier than he had expected. He sent over the information to his technology team and in a few minutes they had an answer for him.

After conveying the news to the police chief, Basler then called Jai, "Mr. Singh, I have news that you will like. Piotr has finally shared his *Evolution* marketplace details and we have now confirmed that he has not communicated any important *Solara* information on the dark net."

"That is such a big relief detective!" exclaimed Jai.

On the crisp Sunday morning Jai enjoyed a large breakfast out on the terrace. Louise enquired about Dev and he told her the encouraging developments.

Jai called Veer to give him further updates on the progress that Dev had been making. Also, that he had spoken when Jai visited him the previous day. There was so much relief in Veer's voice when he said, "As you can imagine, Lalita and I have been waiting on tenterhooks all this while. This is awesome news! How long is the recovery? When can he get discharged from the hospital?"

"It could be several days or weeks depending on how his recuperation proceeds. We just have to take it one day at a time."

"That's fine, as long as he keeps making progress."

Jai then told him about the puzzling *Soomjam* situation. "Naturally we are suspecting that it was someone at the showing. Nobody outside of that group and the household staff really knew that the jewel was in the chalet. So the switch happened around the time of the showing."

"Well that is only logical," responded Veer.

"And I guess I should have listened to you when you tried to tell me about the wisdom of bringing the jewel to the chalet."

After his chat with Veer, Jai called Sophie to tell her that Gauri was planning to come over from Antwerp to be with Dev for a few days.

"Oh that would be nice," responded Sophie, "While she is with Dev, why don't you head out to Zermatt next weekend."

"Well that's what Gauri had also suggested. How about you? It would be wonderful if you came along too?"

"I think that's sounds very exciting! Let's make it work. Do you want to leave Friday evening or Saturday morning?"

"Then let's leave Friday evening. Gauri is planning to be here Friday noon," said Jai, "I will call her and confirm the plan."

Alex received an encrypted message from Gaston. "Jai Singh will be travelling with his girlfriend to Zermatt coming Friday evening. They will drive in his car till Tasch and then take the train from there."

"Ok let me plan accordingly," replied Alex.

"You will not need to use the fake jewel I sent you; please get rid of it," added Gaston.

"Ok," responded Alex.

Leonid Batcheff had worked on the *Solara* synopsis over the weekend and early Monday. He called Sergei around 11 am to confirm that the synopsis seemed genuine.

Sergei had already worked out a plan to reduce the risk for FSB on the half million dollar payout. He realized that even if Leonid had confirmed that the initial data was real, there was still no guarantee that the subsequent information would be genuine.

The proposal he had in mind was that of the five remaining files, Piotr would need to upload them one at a time. Once he uploaded the first file, this would get validated by Leonid and his team. Upon confirmation that the content looked genuine one fifth of the payment would be made. Likewise for the other files, one at a time. This way the risk would be reduced for both the parties.

There would be marginally higher risk for Piotr as he would need to upload the file prior to being paid. But in Sergei's mind this seemed reasonable.

Sergei lost no time in sending his proposal to Piotr on *Evolution*. He was unaware that Piotr had been apprehended by the police.

The Canton of Vaud police technology team continued to monitor Piotr's *Evolution* account. They saw a message come in and promptly relayed it to Basler.

Even though the message was anonymous, Basler was quite sure it was from Moscow. He was happy that he had kept the news of Piotr's capture under wraps.

After working from home the previous week, Jai started attending office in Lausanne. He had a packed morning schedule with several back to back meetings. Around lunch he went over to meet Pierre to talk about the Russian involvement in the *Solara* affair.

Later, he called Basler and said, "I have been able to discuss the Moscow connection with Pierre. It would be good if the three of us could meet in Lausanne sometime today or tomorrow."

"How about if I come down today at 4.30 pm?" said Basler. "I too have some further news on that."

At the appointed hour, Basler was shown into the meeting room where Jai and Pierre were already seated. Jai started by thanking Basler for coming down to Lausanne.

"Detective, so we know that the Russians initiated the data theft for *Solara*. There is no guarantee that they will stop pursuing their efforts."

"That is true," said Basler, "In fact, just this morning a message came in on Piotr's *Evolution* account which we believe is from Moscow. They are willing to pay a half million dollars for the *Solara* information."

"Pierre and I are of the opinion that we should give the Russians what they want," said Jai and looked at Pierre who nodded his head, before turning back to Basler.

Basler threw a confused look at both the scientists who now had broad grins on their faces.

"Let me explain," said Jai, "around four years ago we were working on a predecessor project called *"Bright Star"* but that project did not produce the desired results and it threw us off the mark by a wide margin which we could not have anticipated. It was after much time, thought and effort that we got on to the right track with *Solara*."

"So let me guess," said Basler with enthusiasm building in his voice, "You want to pass along the *Bright Star* information to Moscow in the guise of *Solara*?"

"Exactly!" said Jai, "this will easily set back our Russian friends by a few years."

"And we would be happy to use that money for research work at the institute," chimed in Pierre.

"Everyone gets what they want!" chuckled Basler.

Basler wanted to clarify something, "Even though I believe the party that sent the anonymous message is Moscow, how do we confirm this?"

"There is a unique part – a specific type of diffusion pump that the party will need to order to make *Bright Star* work. The pump is made by a specialist vendor in France. If we keep an ear to the ground in the days ahead, we can learn who has ordered that."

"Looks like you guys have an answer for everything," smiled Basler, "And of course in my official capacity I directly cannot help you. But if you were to somehow get Piotr's log in details the rest would be easy."

His grin became even wider.

The *Bright Star* information was divided into five files, it was transmitted through the *Evolution* site one file at a time over a span of about 8 hours. Upon validation by Leonid's team for each file, one hundred thousand dollars was transmitted five times by Sergei's team.

The payment was made in bitcoins. By Tuesday evening it was confirmed that a diffusion pump was ordered by a party in Moscow.

Upon the satisfactory conclusion of the transaction Jai informed Basler of the results. With this affair being concluded, Basler felt there was no need to provide Jai with the police protection and called it off.

Later, Basler spoke with Dhéry to update her on the events of the past few days. "The *Solara* matter is now laid to rest," said Basler.

"This is good news Jean-Phillipe!"

"Yes Josiane, but we still have the *Soomjam* issue to resolve."

"I am sure you will crack that quite quickly," said Dhéry and continued, "From my side, let me call Radoslaw and tell him to release Igor's goons. Quite a character our Polish friend!"

Dev was making very good progress with his recovery. He was now able to speak short sentences and was also able to sit up for a few minutes. Though his head wound had healed a lot; he still had a dull throb, which was pronounced each time he moved his head. The doctor believed that the pain would be gone in a couple weeks.

Jai came around in the evening and spent some time with him. They talked about Gauri's visit on Friday. "I will be so happy to meet her," said Dev.

"She is here for a whole week, so you will really be able to catch up a lot and remember the good times in Dhawalpur," said Jai.

"I hope Sophie and you enjoy your Zermatt getaway," said Dev trying to grin, "I am glad you have finally started listening to my advice."

"Ok tiger, with all the talk you are able to make, I think you are in the hospital just for the pretty nurses," teased Jai.

Gauri's flight to Geneva was delayed by twenty minutes, she managed to reach Jai's office in Lausanne by 1.30 pm. He was planning to take a half day off and they had planned to travel together to Montreux from there.

"Jai, is it just me or you look ten years older from three weeks ago?" asked a concerned Gauri.

"We will fix all of that with a stopover in Lavaux to pick up all the wine they have," joked Jai.

On a more serious note he continued, "Gauri, the last one week was rather harrowing, especially with Dev's precarious condition, theft of the project data and also the missing *Soomjam*. Mercifully the first two are now under control."

They stopped in Lavaux for lunch and picked up a few bottles of Reserve Noire Grand Cru which Sophie liked. Shortly thereafter, they were back on the Autoroute headed to Montreux with the usual Friday traffic on A9.

"What time are Sophie and you leaving?" asked Gauri.

"We were thinking we will have tea with you and leave around 6 pm. It depends on the traffic, but I think we will get to Tasch by 8 pm, well before it is dark. We will park at Tasch station and take the train into Zermatt from there. We should be in the hotel before 9 pm."

"Hope you guys have a lovely time. Do not worry about Dev, I am looking forward to being with him. Henri and Louise are already here, so I will be in good hands as well."

Her phone rang and she said, "Hello Pranav, I am with Jai, we had a lovely lunch and are now driving back to the chalet."

"That's perfect," he said, "What time is Jai planning to leave?"

"About six in the evening".

"Enjoy your stay and give my regards to your brothers".

When they reached the chalet, Henri and Louise gave Gauri a blow by blow account of the day the robbery happened. They had been upset for many days, but were now happy that Dev was doing better.

Later Sophie came down to the chalet to meet Gauri and joined them for tea on the terrace. They sat together sipping the delicately flavored Darjeeling brew that Louise had served. Later it was time for Jai and Sophie to be on their way to Zermatt.

It was while he was in Paris that Alex had already done his homework. He had gone over the maps and decided that the best place to execute his plan was going to be after Jai exited Autoroute A9 and drove along the narrower mountain roads between Stalden and Tasch.

Alex reached Switzerland on Thursday morning and had checked into a hotel in Lausanne. He then spent the better part of Thursday afternoon driving along the twenty kilometer stretch between Stalden and Tasch. He settled upon a double hairpin bend just before the small town of Randa. He thoroughly examined the ridge and found it met his expectations.

Jai's bright yellow Maserati would be easy to spot from a distance. Once it negotiated the first hairpin bend, Alex planned to bump Jai's car off the road and plunge it into the deep ridge that plummeted two hundred feet down.

Using his mountaineering skills, he would then descend to where Jai's car had fallen to make sure that he and his girlfriend were dead. If they happened to survive the fall, he would take care of that very easily.

He would need two vehicles to execute his plan. Through his contacts in Switzerland he had found an auto repair shop in Lausanne that would loan him their roadside assistance truck for a day. He had agreed to pay them twenty five thousand dollars in cash. The truck would serve several important purposes.

One, he would park it on the road at the first hairpin bend with the emergency flashers on. This would force Jai to slow down and swerve his car in the direction of the ridge; giving Alex the opportunity to strike from behind with his Range Rover. By using sufficient force he would manage to send the Maserati into the gorge. A roadside assistance truck was the perfect choice of vehicle to use, as it would not raise any suspicions of any motorists driving by.

Second, he would use the truck to transport his Range Rover to and from the site. It would be very likely that the Range Rover would get damaged after the planned accident with Jai. Putting it on the flat bed of the truck would allow him the opportunity to get away without suspicion. The garage had also agreed to repair his vehicle upon his return to Lausanne.

Sophie looked radiant in her chic navy and white sports skirt and polo shirt. She looked forward to being with Jai on this mini vacation. She knew the past two weeks had been tough on him, but in part this had also been the reason for them coming closer together.

Zermatt would be great fun, even though the snow at this time of the year was far less than during the winter season. The place itself always looked so welcoming, set in a lush valley surrounded by tall mountains. It was dominated by the Matterhorn to the southwest and the beautiful Mattervispa river flowed through the town.

On their drive, Jai seemed quite relaxed. A big burden had been lifted from his chest now that he knew that his years of painstaking research was no longer in jeopardy of being in the wrong hands. He and Sophie spoke about their lives. It had been a long while since they had been together and there was some bit of catching up to do.

Since Jai trusted Sophie, he told her about the *Bright Star* information they had shared with Moscow. She was quite amused to hear how they had managed to dupe the Russians.

"So what happens when the Russians find out they went on a wild goose chase?" she asked.

"Well it will take them a few years to realize that. In any case they believe they got the information from Piotr, who they will think copied the wrong data from my laptop," responded Jai.

By the time they left the main highway, the conversation veered towards the mystery of the missing *Soomjam*. Jai frowned and became a bit despondent. The thought of losing the family heirloom was disconcerting. Would the police be able to recover it?

Sophie sensed his feelings and reached out to take his hands in hers as the car moved smoothly down the road.

Alex was on his way to Randa when he got a secure message from Gaston confirming that Jai and Sophie were starting for Zermatt at 6 pm. Alex knew that they would reach the hairpin bend around 7.50 pm. At 7.30 pm he parked the truck at the first hairpin with its emergency lights on. He got into his Range Rover which was in the back of the truck and putting it in reverse, he backed out. He then parked his car a few hundred meters before the bend on the shoulder and bided his time.

He was lucky, there was no traffic on the road. After about 15 minutes of patiently waiting, he saw a car looking tiny in the rear view mirror and became more alert. As it neared, Alex could see the yellow car quite clearly. It crossed him and slowed a little before the bend. Alex, who had his engine running, speeded up to catch the Maserati.

While Jai was familiar with the hairpin bend as he had done the journey several times, he was not anticipating a parked truck which was not visible beforehand. As the truck suddenly came in view, he had to slam his brakes and turn sharply to avoid the truck. Just then, the speeding Range Rover struck the Maserati from behind with great force.

Even as Jai slammed the brakes, the Maserati went through the guard rail ripping the metal off the guard post. The car screeched to a stop just a few feet from the edge of the ridge. The edges of the torn railing lay at an outward angle away from the road. Sophie screamed and was blue with fright. Jai realized they had escaped death by a hair's breadth, but the danger was not over as they were precariously close to the cliff's edge. Losing no time Jai rapidly engaged the car in reverse.

Alex realized that he had narrowly missed sending Jai over the cliff. He speedily backed his car and pressed on the accelerator. Just one harder hit on Jai's car and the job would be accomplished. As the Range Rover surged forward he saw the Maserati moving back. The torn guard rail caught on the Maserati bumper and swung towards Alex' windshield. He had no option but to swerve to avoid the railing. It was already too late, the railing struck the glass and smashed inside to rip the side of his face off. As the Range Rover swerved, it hit the Maserati at an angle and caused Jai's car to dangle dangerously at the edge of the precipice. The Range Rover rolled forward a few meters, hit the guard rail post and came to a stop.

Jai knew that they were in a perilous situation, one wrong move and they could plunge into the gorge. He pulled the handbrake hard to stabilize the car and looked across to make sure that Sophie was unhurt. Sophie looked stunned and white in the face. She was now crying and the nails of her left hand had dug grooves in his thigh. Jai reassured her that everything would be fine and asked her to step out gently. Sophie was petrified and unable to move an inch. Jai's gentle but firm voice gave her the needed courage. With great caution she opened the door and stepped out gingerly. Once she was outside the car, Jai opened his door and very slowly got out himself. He walked round and hugged Sophie tightly who was still in shock. He then dialed the emergency number.

When Sophie was a little steadier, Jai sat her down on the side and walked over to the Range Rover. He could see that the driver had not survived the crash. The engine of the car was still running.

Pranav called Gaston around 10 pm. He was getting very frustrated as there was no news from Alex.

"Pranav, he uses a secure tool, maybe he does not have a connection now, let us wait some more time," said Gaston.

It was around 11 pm when Gauri's phone rang. Pranav braced himself to hear the news. Gauri seemed to be in great shock. She related the news about Jai and Sophie's accident and their narrow escape from death. Then she mentioned that the other driver was dead, leaving Pranav in a state of shock.

Somehow he managed to mumble, "Thank god Jai and Sophie are well! I am looking forward to meeting you all next Saturday," conveying the relief that he did not feel.

Upon hanging up, he called Gaston who was astounded to learn of the sequence of events. He had so much faith in Alex that he had a hard time digesting the news.

"Can they trace it back to us?" asked Pranav.

"No they cannot, the messages were exchanged using an encrypted tool. Also, we have not made any payments that can be traced back," Gaston assured him.

"Ok, perhaps we can lie low for some time and finish the job at the appropriate time."

"Mon ami, you do seem very intent in getting rid of your brother in law!"

The next day Pranav took out the jewel from the office safe and sent it via courier to an overseas destination.

After the harrowing ordeal, Jai and Sophie had been in no mood to proceed to Zermatt and decided to return home to the chalet. The police had taken their statements and had moved the car safely back to the road. Though the rear bumper and fender were damaged, the car was still drivable.

When they reached the chalet, Gauri had already come back after meeting Dev in the hospital and was surprised to see them return home. They had decided not to call her and convey the news on phone. It was very disconcerting for Gauri to listen to them describe what had transpired.

At breakfast the next day, the three sat together on the terrace discussing the recent spate of events. The mood was quite grey as they talked about what had happened. Or, what could have happened.

Around mid-day Saturday, Basler came over to the chalet with some further information about the accident the previous evening. He had already spoken with the Valais County police under whose jurisdiction the incident had taken place.

"Have you ever met or seen the driver of the car that slammed into you before?" Basler started off with a question.

"I could not see his face properly as it was getting a bit dark and he was quite badly injured. But to the best of my recollection I have never seen him," Jai responded.

"His name is Alex Black who lived in Paris and was a professional assassin." said Basler.

The news sent a chill down the spines of the three sitting with the detective.

"The plan was very diabolical. If he was successful in pushing your car down the gorge, this case may have been unresolved. There were no witnesses as the road was deserted and there would not have been any evidence of any wrongdoing," continued Basler.

His words brought no comfort to the three listening to him.

"Why do you think there would not have been any evidence?" asked Sophie, shuddering at the macabre thought.

"He would simply have put his Range Rover on the truck and covered the car to hide it from sight and transported it back to the garage for repairs. He would then have driven back to Paris and nobody would have known anything."

"But what about the Maserati, would the damage to the bumper not have revealed the cause of the accident?" asked Jai.

"After dropping into the steep gorge several hundred feet, it is very unlikely that much could have been found or discerned," said Basler.

"So who do you think hired him and for what purpose?" was her next worried question.

"I think this is related to the *Soomjam* affair. But we cannot yet connect the dots, we are analyzing all his telephone calls, nothing has emerged yet. We are continuing to investigate and I will be going to Paris to coordinate with the police there," said Basler.

"How safe is Jai, will they not try again?" asked a concerned Gauri.

"We are not sure of that, but I am reinstating the police protection for Jai again, two armed men to be around him at all times," said Basler.

Dev had made great progress and was released from hospital. Jai, Gauri and Sophie went down to pick him up. His headache had disappeared by now and he was feeling quite cheerful. He would still need to use a wheelchair to move around but he was able to talk cogently.

"Ok Prince, time to go, you seem to be getting all the attention, other patients are getting neglected," jested Sophie.

"Only on one condition my lovely, if you promise to sit with me all day instead of with Jai, I am prepared to leave," chortled Dev. Sophie laughed and give him an affectionate peck on the cheek.

When he got home, Louise would pop in every half an hour to check how he was doing and if he wanted to eat or drink something.

Veer and Lalita called and spoke to Dev at length. They were overjoyed with the improvement in his condition. They promised to come down to Montreux in a few weeks' time to visit him.

Gauri and Sophie sat with him and updated him on the progress of the entire case. He was happy to learn that his assailant, Piotr, was behind bars. They also told him of the Alex Black affair. This news was quite distressing to Dev.

To lighten the mood, Jai brought out the Suntory whiskey that Dev had carried and promised to open it soon. But for that he would need to recover more as he was still on antibiotics.

In the evening, Nicole dropped by and offered to make him Swiss Barley Soup. Dev told her that she would need to first have a battle with Louise and win over the kitchen before she could think of making anything. Everybody laughed at the joke and also knowing that Dev was getting back in his element.

It was after dinner that Basler called Jai to let him know that he was back from Paris.

"Any further progress?" asked Jai.

"I am afraid there is not much to report yet. I am hoping to receive some information from London tomorrow. Also, I will be speaking with someone that attended the showing," said Basler.

"Detective, we have a get together at my place on Saturday evening, mainly family and close friends, but it would be wonderful if you could join us for the occasion," requested Jai.

"I would be most delighted to attend," said Basler.

Pranav landed at Geneva at about 3 pm and he was in Montreux by 4.30 pm. Despite the fiasco with Alex Black, he felt quite confident about how things had progressed. The fake *Soomjam* was lost to sea and there was nothing to connect him with Alex. He planned on having a good time at the chalet.

At dinner it would be a small gathering and apart from family members, there were Sophie, Nicole and Detective Basler. There was a lot of merriment in the air as they celebrated not only Jai's birthday but also Dev's homecoming.

They were all seated in the well-appointed dining room and were served by Henri. Louise had prepared delicious Indian Mughlai food. There were succulent lamb kababs, chicken korma, butter dal, delicately roasted potatoes with fenugreek, cucumber raita and soft tandoor roasted naans. For Basler, it was cuisine he had not tried before and he could not stop praising the cook.

After dinner, it was time to cut the cake. Gauri had ordered a delicious chocolate mousse from the best local bakery. As Jai blew out the candle, they all sang for him. Later, as they sat around sipping port, Jai announced, "I want to thank all of you for making my day special," then he turned to look at the detective and raised his glass, "But I do want to particularly thank Detective Basler for his superior work on the case."

"Yes, one part of the investigation was a success, but so far, the other part has been hanging fire," said Basler. "There were two things robbed that day. Some very important information from Jai's computer, and of course *Soomjam*. With information from MI6 and help from French police, we were very effective in wrapping up the case relating to information theft."

He continued, "But I wanted to utilize this opportunity today to provide an update on where we stand on *Soomjam* and related events," said Basler.

"It is a shame that the jewel is lying at the bottom of the sea," said Pranav with a hint of smirk in his voice.

Basler's voice turned serious, "No, it is not," he said, taking it out of his pocket and placing it on the table. "As a matter of fact it was never lost in the sea. But yes, it is shameful that what we have here is a fake!"

There was pin drop silence in the room. Pranav could feel the tension inside but kept his composure.

Basler continued, "We already know that the jewel was switched at the time of the showing. After the theft, we naturally investigated the people that had attended the showing but our initial findings were inconclusive."

"Then it was time to focus on the family and household staff. In fact, these were the people with most access and opportunity. I am of course talking about Jai, Gauri, Pranav, Henri and Louise. We checked out all the leads but unfortunately did not find anything at all."

"We ran an analysis on the fake jewel to see if we could identify anything, but found nothing to help identify the culprit."

Hearing this Pranav relaxed a little.

"Detective, how about Alex and your visit to Paris? Were you able to find anything there?" asked Jai.

"We ran a thorough check on Alex' communications, but the parties used an encryption tool. Neither were there any recent payments in his accounts. So no luck there."

Pranav silently thanked Gaston for using secure communications. He felt the tension melt away some more.

Then Basler said, "We checked his apartment and found a package but the contents were gone."

Pranav congratulated himself for asking Gaston to have Alex get rid of the second fake.

"An empty package? How would that help you?" asked Gauri.

"That is something that got us stumped," said Basler.

Good thing, Gaston used a complicated route to send the package, thought Pranav. Even though things seemed to be working for him presently, this detective was like a basset hound who would not give up. He decided that he would return to Antwerp, take care of some monetary transactions and disappear for good.

Jai poured everyone more port. Dev complained that he did not get a second round. "You are under medication, my friend, and so feel lucky that you got one drink," was Jai's retort.

Basler continued, "Allow me to continue with what happened next. So even though we got stuck initially, we had no choice but to involve MI6 as the package seemed to have been routed through London. MI6 used their network to track the package and we were able to trace it to its origin." Basler paused here for dramatic effect.

The level of tension in the room ratcheted up several notches and everyone stared at Basler.

"The sender was Gaston Collard from Antwerp," it was Basler's turn to stare at Pranav.

"Are you suggesting that Gaston did all this on his own?" asked Pranav, tightness rising in his chest.

"No sir! We also investigated the telephone calls made between Jai and Gauri about his trip to Zermatt and corresponded those with your calls to your partner, Gaston. There is a strong correlation which clearly establishes your own link to Alex Black."

Pranav knew he was caught. He snatched a hunting knife from the wall and held it on Dev's throat. "Anyone move and I slit his throat."

He motioned Dev to wheel himself outside the room and held the knife to his back as they moved up to the door.

As soon as Dev had moved past the door, his wheelchair was grabbed and pulled aside by one of the two armed police officers stationed outside. Just then, Jai, who had gotten up and walked behind Pranav, landed him a blow from behind.

Pranav turned around and lunged at Jai with the knife, who caught his hand and twisted it hard such that the knife clattered to the floor. The other officer pointed his gun at Pranav, who tried to make a run for it. After a brief chase they caught him and put him in handcuffs.

"Pranav Rana you are under arrest!" said Basler proudly, "You committed your crime here; poetic justice has prevailed that you are caught right here in Switzerland."

Sophie and Nicole tried to comfort Gauri, but she was more angry than sorrowful, "Pranav, you did all this to make some money? But what depravity led you to think of murder?"

"Injustice!" hissed Pranav.

"Let me explain," said Basler in a grave tone. "We learnt about Pranav's connection to *Soomjam* on Wednesday. So we contacted the Indian authorities the day before and found out that it was, in fact, Pranav's cousin that was suspected of the 2004 attempt to steal *Soomjam*. Since there was no proof, the matter just faded away in time."

Everybody not only appeared astonished but also confused.

"Looks like the Ranas of Kedarnagar still bear a grudge after 150 years!" stated Basler.

"We managed to finish off your parents in the plane crash, we are not done, we will prevail over Dhawalpur!" blurted Pranav.

It was sheer gentleman's gallantry that prevented Jai from striking a man in handcuffs as he seethed inside hearing the cruel fact. He thought for a moment as the implications set in, "This is hurtful but I am glad the truth of the Ranas is out, we will now make sure that justice will prevail."

Basler turned to his audience and said gravely, "This man should get the most severe punishment permissible under law. Honestly, my evidence was still circumstantial, but I am happy that I was able to force his hand."

"Detective, your trap did work quite well. We are all glad this is behind us now," said Jai.

"In all of this, are we not missing something vital?" asked Dev shaking off his bewilderment, "Where is *Soomjam*?"

Sitting on a chair with his handcuffs and the policemen standing at guard next to him, Pranav sneered at them all and said, "I have already dispatched the jewel to a safe location, you will never find it! At least I have that satisfaction."

There was a look of dismay and disappointment on most faces in the room.

"Even on that account Mr. Rana, you were not successful," declared Basler and proceeded to take out the real *Soomjam* from his other pocket with great flourish. The large sapphire glittered and dazzled and the diamonds flashed brilliantly under the chandelier lights. There was a big gasp from everybody sitting in the room.

The detective beamed as he turned to look at Nicole and said, "And for this, my dear, should I arrest you or thank you?"

Nicole laughed and held up her hands, "You could thank Sir John, I guess. I just did what he asked me to do," she said self-effacingly.

"Could somebody explain all this please?" pleaded Gauri, who had recovered sufficiently by now.

"Allow me to do so", said Nicole. "You see, when Veer heard about the showing at the chalet, he was anxious that someone may attempt to steal it. So he expressed his concern to Sir John, someone he could trust. They discussed the list of people who would be attending. I was on the list, so Sir John called me and explained the situation; and requested my help to which I agreed. He had a replica created and asked me to replace it with the original at the time of the showing. Fortunately, the plan worked and I was able to replace the original with the fake on the day of the showing. So the one that Pranav stole later was the fake I had planted!"

Pranav could barely believe what he was hearing, all color drained from his face as he sat there looking dazed. He now recalled that he had not even seen the jewel after stealing it. He had been sure of its authenticity.

Jai turned to Basler and asked, "So Detective, when did you come to know about this?"

Basler responded, "You see, during our investigations I had known that Nicole had opened a new bank locker the day after the showing. At first we had brushed it aside thinking it was unrelated to the events. But after Piotr's capture, when the fake came to light, we doubled our efforts on all the attendees of the showing. Finally, on Wednesday I spoke with Nicole about the locker and she confided about her role and that the real jewel was lying safe in that very locker."

"I requested Nicole to maintain her silence as we were still investigating Pranav and Gaston, and we agreed that we would carry

Soomjam to the dinner today and lift the veil once and for all. So here we are," finished Basler triumphantly.

"But Nicole why did you not come forward when the news of *Soomjam* theft came out initially?" asked Gauri.

"Sir John requested that I keep it under wraps so as not to diminish the impact of the ongoing investigation," said Nicole.

Basler gestured to the policemen to take Pranav away. When he was gone, there was a sense of merriment and cheer in the room and Jai poured another round for all. Dev got a small drink as well.

Jai could not help himself, he turned to Gauri and observed, "You guys were together ten years, I never realized he was a double Rana."

"Now what does that mean?" asked Gauri.

"Parse his first name (P-rana-v) and you'll see!" grinned Jai.

Sir John sat in his library sipping a cognac under the portrait of a majestic looking soldier in full military attire. He picked up the phone as it rang, it was Veer calling from Dhawalpur.

"John, thanks for taking a personal interest in this whole matter," said Veer, pulling on his pipe.

"No thanks needed, Veer," replied Sir John modestly.

"Of course appreciation is in order here. You helped on three critical fronts, tipping off about the data theft, keeping *Soomjam* secure and tracking the package back to Pranav, because of which we learnt about the Rana intrigue," said Veer.

"My friend, we go back a long way, I had to do everything I could," said Sir John, raising his glass to the portrait of his maternal forebear behind him.

Inscribed below the portrait were the words "General Patrick Howarth, Commander of the 4th Battalion, British Army in India".

About the Author

Kunal Mohanlal moved from New Delhi to the US in the 90s and lives in New Jersey with his wife and two sons. He is an Engineer and MBA and has worked in Banking and Financial Technology segment for over two decades.

He considers himself to be an accidental author as this profession was never intended. But his vivid imagination and love for a thrilling suspense inspired him to express himself in this, his maiden novella "The Steal: An Adventure in Montreux".

He loves the company of his friends, traveling, reading and watching shows and movies. He especially enjoys adventure and mystery. His favorite shows are Poirot, Sherlock, Wallander and Lilyhammer.